HARD

CELL

PAUL ORTON

Copyright © 2023 Paul Orton

The right of Paul Orton to be identified as the Author of the Work has been asserted by him in accordance with the Copyright, Designs and Patents Act 1988.
All rights reserved.

Apart from any use permitted under UK copyright law, this publication may only be reproduced, stored or transmitted, in any form, or by any means with prior permission in writing from the copyright holder or in the case of reprographic production in accordance with the terms of licences issued by the Copyright Licensing Agency and may not be otherwise circulated in any form of binding or cover other than that in which it is published and without a similar condition being imposed on the subsequent purchaser.

All characters in this publication are fictitious and any resemblance to real persons, living or dead, is purely co-incidental.

Font used for front cover, titles and chapter headings: 'Hacked' © David Libeau, used under Creative Commons Licence.

"If people are good only because they fear punishment, and hope for reward, then we are a sorry lot indeed."

Albert Einstein

PROL(

CW01500178

'Ever wanted a tattoo, Ryan?'

His captor walked towards him with a long needle.

Ryan struggled in the chair, but the straps held him tight. He could barely speak. 'No.'

'That's a shame, because you're about to get one. Right here on your forehead. Can you guess what it's going to be?'

Ryan squirmed.

How could he have been so stupid?

'I don't know.'

'I'll give you a clue. Only boys have them.'

Ryan swore. 'Not that. Anything but that.'

'Don't worry, Ryan. I'm sure you'll be able to get it removed eventually, when you're released from Blackfell. You'll only have to put up with it for a few years.'

Ryan wanted to throw up.

His enemy had him exactly where he wanted him, and no-one would come to his rescue.

'Please… Don't do it.'

Ryan's captor smirked. 'Do you know how pathetic you sound? I haven't even started yet. Now, hold still. I'm afraid this *is* going to hurt.'

1. DESPAIR

Ryan wiped sweat from his forehead.

He did it with his left hand; his right was handcuffed to a metal bar.

The prison van bumped violently as it made its way along the country lanes. They drove past green trees and a sparkling river, but the scenery didn't put Ryan at ease.

He knew where they were taking him: Blackfell. A secure military facility for young offenders.

A metal grille separated him from the driver and the special agent that accompanied him. They didn't speak, and if Ryan said anything, they threatened to gag him. He was uncomfortable enough as it was, so he stayed silent.

He'd been dragged out of the hospital and was only wearing pyjama trousers. His top half was still naked and his back stuck to the torn leather of the seat. There was no air conditioning, and even though the driver had his window open, hardly any of the breeze made it to where he was sitting.

He was being transported like a convict.

No, wait, he *was* a convict.

His life was over.

He'd be locked up at Blackfell for years, with no

access to a computer and no hope of release. Even by his standards, this was bad.

It's not fair.

That was true. For once, he didn't deserve it. Everyone thought he was guilty of releasing a virus that shut down military systems, killing pilots as aircraft plummeted to the ground.

But he wasn't.

Ryan had discovered the actual cause of the shutdown and stopped it, but the evil genius Conrad Wolff had framed him, and forced him to make a false confession. The worst part was that even his closest friends thought he'd betrayed them.

Ryan wiped away a tear as he stared out the window. The agent in the front seat glanced back at him. 'Not so cocky now, eh?'

Ryan glared at him.

'Don't worry,' continued the man. 'They'll soon knock that attitude out of you at Blackfell. By the time you've spent a few days there, you'll be a changed boy. It'll all be *yes, sir, no, sir.*'

'I'm terrified,' shot back Ryan.

The agent didn't respond, but instead turned to the driver. 'See, they're gonna have a *lot* of fun with this one.'

Somehow, that didn't make Ryan feel any better.

***

Woodland gave way to a much bleaker landscape of hills covered in rocks and dry bracken. Ryan couldn't remember the last time he'd seen a village or a farmhouse.

After a while, a stupidly high steel fence blocked their way. At the top were several coils of barbed wire.

'Reckon you could climb that?' asked the agent.

Ryan grunted and looked away.

'I didn't think so. Take your last look at the free world. It's going to be some time before you see it again.'

Ryan gulped. He was still trying to put on a brave face, but the man was right. He had no idea how long it would be before they let him out.

It could be years.

A gate opened to let them through. On the other side were more gates, more fences. The place was a fortress.

You'll never escape.

The sun was still shining, but nothing looked as bright. The ground was all brown dirt and moss. They passed a tired basketball court surrounded by another fence. Here, even sport was played in a cage.

Up ahead were a few grey concrete buildings with bars on the windows.

So far, they hadn't seen any people. Were they all inside? How many kids even ended up in a place like this?

As they drew close to the buildings, the prison van came to a stop. The agent climbed into the back and uncuffed him.

Ryan stepped out, the tarmac burning his bare feet. He glanced around. There was nowhere to run.

The door to the building opened and two dark figures

came out. They were dressed in black combats like they belonged in the SAS, but they also wore helmets with mirrored visors, so he couldn't see their faces.

One of them held a long silver stick in his hand. It was probably a metal detector to check Ryan hadn't got anything hidden on him. They hardly needed to do that; all he was wearing was pyjama trousers.

'Here's the transfer paperwork.' The driver handed over a clipboard. 'We need a signature here.'

One of the dark figures scrawled something and passed it back. The driver and special agent climbed back into the van. They were gone so fast that Ryan got the impression even they were eager to escape. That left him alone with the faceless prison guards.

'Come with us.' The voice was metallic, inhuman. Ryan had to give it to them: whoever had designed these outfits had done a great job.

'What if I don't?' said Ryan. Part of him wanted to go inside, just to escape the scorching sun, but he didn't like being ordered around.

The man didn't answer the question. Instead, he raised the metal stick and prodded Ryan on the stomach. An electric shock coursed through his body, making him yell and step back. 'Hey, you can't do that!'

'Come with us.' The guard lifted the stick again, making it clear that he would have no hesitation in electrocuting Ryan all the way to the open door.

Ryan shuffled forward, his heart thudding.

These guys were serious.

This place was intense.

And he was already out of his depth.

2. SCHEDULE

The first room was empty. Old white chipped tiles covered the walls, reminding him of the changing rooms at Devonmoor.

'Stand there.' The soldier pointed at the far wall. Ryan knew what would happen if he didn't, so he obeyed.

'What now?' he asked, trying to sound like he wasn't scared, but not quite managing to hide his fear.

'Remove your clothes.'

'Here?'

'Yes.'

'In front of you?'

The man raised the stick and stepped forward.

Ryan backed away. 'I was just asking.'

Feeling self-conscious, Ryan turned to face the wall and pulled off his pyjama bottoms. He threw them on the ground where the guard flicked them aside with the baton.

Ryan realised that even though it was still hot in here, he was shivering. These men could do anything, and he couldn't stop them.

'Remain where you are.'

Ryan waited, glancing over his shoulder.

The men stood on the other side of the room, making

sure he didn't move. Seconds later, he found out why.

Jets of water shot out from the walls and ceiling, hitting his body from every direction. It was freezing. Whichever way he moved, he couldn't escape.

He spluttered as it made its way up his nostrils; it felt like someone had pointed a hose at his face.

'That's enough!' he shouted. 'Make it stop!'

The guards ignored him, waiting until the jets shut off by themselves. Ryan hugged his body, trying to stop his teeth from chattering.

'This way,' ordered the guard. He opened a door. 'In here.'

Ryan stumbled through. Another tiled room, this time with a bench. On it was a green towel and a pile of clothes.

'Get dressed.'

This time, the men walked out, leaving him alone.

The towel was as rough as sandpaper, but he didn't care; it didn't take long to get dry. He was grateful to have proper clothes to wear, even though it was all army gear: camo trousers, a tight green t-shirt, thick green boot socks. Instead of army boots, they'd given him some black canvas slip-on shoes.

After months at Devonmoor, Ryan was used to wearing strange uniforms. It was clean and it almost fitted. That was all that mattered.

Once he was dressed, he tried the door the soldiers had left through, but it was locked. He knocked tentatively. 'I'm ready.'

Nothing.

He sat down on the bench.

***

They made him wait.

Maybe it was all part of the torture, having him sweat it out, imagining every possible scenario?

He hated to admit it, but it worked. He was desperate to find out what would happen next, what this place was like.

Eventually, the door opened, and the guards reappeared. 'This way.'

The next room was small and black, with no windows and no furniture. As the door closed, they were in complete darkness. The guards stood behind him, uncomfortably close.

Then, something lit up in front of him: a screen.

An image appeared: a silhouette of a man's face against a dark blue background.

'Prisoner, welcome to Blackfell. I'm the governor here, but like all of our staff, I prefer to remain anonymous.'

That wasn't a good sign.

'Why?' asked Ryan. The word was barely out of his mouth before the baton was jammed into his back, sending electricity coursing through his body. He cried out in pain.

'You will learn respect here. That's one reason you have been sent to us. You speak only when asked a question. You begin and end every sentence with the word *sir*. Do you understand?'

'Yes, *sir*.' Another shock. Ryan turned on the guard.

'What was that for?'

The guard jabbed again, and as another jolt of electricity made its way through his body, Ryan dropped to the floor, cowering away from the baton.

The governor repeated his last words. 'You begin and end every sentence with the word *sir*. Do you understand?'

Now Ryan got it. 'Sir, yes, sir.' His voice trembled.

The guard withdrew the baton.

'Get up.'

Ryan stood, very aware of the stick to his right.

'I've read your file, prisoner. I know that you're a rebel. It will take some time to adjust to life here, but you will get used to it. You see, every day here is the same. Every single day. There are no weekends, no holidays, no days off.'

No weekends? No holidays?

Ryan hadn't thought about the fact that he'd no longer see his parents at the end of term, and he realised just how much he'd miss them.

'There are no computers here either, so your hacking skills won't be of any use. As you'll discover, we're somewhat *old-fashioned* in our approach to education.'

Ryan couldn't imagine what it would be like to live in a place with no technology.

The governor continued: 'Just so we are clear: you are going to be in this institution for years. There is no hope of release, and no escape. Blackfell is tough. Even if you follow the rules, your time here will be miserable. If you don't... well, I wouldn't recommend finding out.'

Ryan could feel his leg shaking. It was like a bad

14

dream. The worst part was, he knew that what the man was saying was true.

Hold on to hope, Ryan.

He couldn't give up. Not yet.

'Prisoner, you belong to me now. Here you will be known as Number Six. Do you understand?'

Ryan almost choked on the words. 'Sir, yes, sir.'

'Good. Then your punishment can begin.'

3. DORM

They herded Ryan along a short corridor like an animal until they reached a large steel door. The guard opened it to reveal a square dormitory, bigger than the ones at Devonmoor, but with less furniture.

Rusty metal bunk beds. Grey brick walls. Dusty concrete floor. One high window with thick steel bars. Five boys, all jumping up to stand to attention as if their lives depended on it, all wearing the same clothes.

And the smell. Ryan was used to sharing a room with other lads, but nothing prepared him for this, even the changing rooms at Devonmoor. It was more like a toilet block than a bedroom. Ryan coughed into his elbow, wanting to puke.

'Your new home.' The guard pushed Ryan in and slammed the door.

'Look who it is. Number Six.' A blond lad with intense blue eyes closed in on him. He was the same age as Ryan, smaller than most of the boys in the dorm.

'I'm Ryan.'

'No, you're Six. You don't get a name.'

Ryan shrugged, not wanting a fight. 'So, who are you? Number One?'

'I'm Three. Give me your clothes.'

'What?' Ryan wasn't sure he'd heard correctly.

'Your clothes. Give them to me.'

The other lads gathered around, and none of them looked friendly. One of them must have been at least sixteen and worked out a lot. He stood at Three's shoulder.

Ryan stalled. 'I'm not sure I'm meant to.'

Three clicked his fingers. The big lad grabbed Ryan by the throat and held him against the wall.

'Let me explain how things work here. Out there, the governor is in charge. In here, I am. If I tell you to do something, you do it. Or you get battered. Understand?'

Ryan nodded. He was in a strange place, outnumbered, with no hope of escape. It wasn't a good time to test boundaries.

'Then give me your clothes.'

Three snapped his fingers again and the big lad let go. Ryan slowly took off his t-shirt, aware that everyone was watching. Three snatched it from him and sniffed it, letting out a deep breath.

'Clean clothes at last,' he said to the others. Then he turned back to Ryan. 'Get a move on.'

Ryan shuffled off his camo trousers and handed them over. 'Happy now?'

Three raised his eyebrows. 'I need your underwear. And your socks.'

Three stripped off, dumping his own clothes in a pile. As soon as Ryan took off his underpants, Three grabbed them and pulled them on, letting out a sigh of pleasure.

'Clean briefs. Such a good feeling.'

'W-W-What do I wear?' asked Ryan, stark naked as

he stood against the wall.

'Those.' Three pointed to the pile on the floor.

Ryan leaned down and retched as he picked the underwear off the top of the pile. 'I can't. They're gross.'

'Put them on or I'll get Four to give you a beating you'll never forget.'

The large lad took one step closer, as if to underline the point.

Ryan swallowed his pride and pulled on the briefs.

'There's a good boy,' soothed Three. 'Now the rest.'

Ryan took the camo trousers off the pile and stepped into them. They were crusty with mud around the knees and backside. But the skinny t-shirt was worse. It was stained and smelt like a stagnant dishcloth.

As he pulled on the socks, he ventured a question. 'Don't you ever get clean clothes?'

'Sure, we do. When we earn them.'

'Or when a new boy arrives,' joked another boy.

'That's not right,' muttered Ryan, horrified. 'It can't be legal.'

'Try complaining to the governor then,' snorted Three. 'See what happens. I dare you.'

The others chuckled as they dispersed back to their bunks, the entertainment over. Ryan noticed one bunk was empty. Presumably that was his. He made his way over.

Three turned on him. 'Did I say you could move?'

'I don't want any trouble.'

'Then get back to the wall and stay there.'

Ryan realised he could be sharing a room with these boys for years. It didn't look promising. He needed to make friends, and fast.

He tried to reason with the boy. 'We're all stuck here, right? Why don't we try to get along? We can be friends.'

The boy shook his head. 'No-one is gonna be your friend, Six. You're an outcast. The entertainment. Get used to it.'

'But why? Just cause I'm new?'

Three shrugged. 'We have our reasons. Now, if you're not against that wall in three seconds, Four is going to use you as a punchbag.'

Ryan backed off. 'Fine, I'm against the wall. Happy now? How long do I have to stay here to pass your initiation?'

Three laughed. 'You think we're hazing you? That's funny. Nah, we're just getting started. If I were you, I'd be grateful when we ignore you. The alternative is much worse.'

Ryan couldn't believe they would be so cruel. 'You know this is what they want, right? For us to torture each other, to make things worse?'

'But we're not torturing each other,' pointed out Three. 'Only you. Me and the other lads get on fine. Now, shut your mouth. I don't want to hear another word.'

Ryan slumped against the wall. He watched as the boys settled down on their bunks. Three was clearly in charge here, despite his size, and none of the others were going to befriend Ryan without his permission.

Why were they being so harsh?

The worst offenders came to Blackfell, and the lads in the dorm didn't look like nice kids. Three had a pinched face and cold eyes. He seemed like the kind of kid that threw stones at cats for fun. Ryan might just be the latest target for his little games.

Or maybe life at Blackfell was so tough it turned all the inmates into horrible people. Perhaps after a few months here, he would hate everyone too?

But there was a slight glimmer of hope. The lads seemed to get on ok with each other. A few were chatting as they lay on their bunks.

'It's so hot,' said one boy, who hadn't spoken before now. He was taller than Three and had hair that reached down to his shoulders.

'PT was murder,' agreed Four, the big lad.

'Still better than February,' pointed out Three. 'I'd rather be too hot than freeze.'

'Maybe if we keep our side of the deal, we'll get some heating installed?' suggested the first kid. 'Could you ask the governor?'

Three shrugged. 'I could ask. Doubt it would ever happen.'

'Worth a try, though.'

Ryan sat against the wall, listening to them talk. His clothes stank and everyone hated him. He wanted to cry, but didn't want to show any sign of weakness.

He'd been in Blackfell for less than an hour, and could already feel his hope draining away.

He needed to turn this situation around.

And fast.

4. TRAY

'I need the toilet.' It was half-true. Ryan hadn't been for hours. But he also wanted to check out the bathroom, to get his bearings and see if there was any hope of escape.

'Do you now?' Three looked up, amused.

'Let him wet himself,' suggested Four.

Please don't do that.

'Nah, we'd only have to smell it for the next month. Toilet is through there.' Three pointed to a shabby wooden door in the corner.

'Thanks.' Ryan didn't know why he was thanking the kid who was bullying him, but he was glad to hear there was at least a toilet in the dorm.

He felt less positive when he saw it. A tiny concrete cubicle without a window. A single metal toilet bowl, with no seat. And it didn't look like it had been cleaned in months. He now knew why the dormitory smelt so bad.

There was a tiny sink with a push-button tap. It only let out a cold dribble, and the moment you let go of the button, even that stopped.

Worse still, there wasn't any toilet roll. Thankfully, right now, he didn't need any. He took a slash and flushed the toilet, and tried to wash his hands in the pathetic excuse of a sink.

There was no way to dry them, so he shook them and wiped them on his trousers as he made his way back into the dorm.

He probably still wasn't meant to speak, but his curiosity got the better of him. 'What happened to the loo roll?'

One boy found the question funny. 'He thinks this is a hotel.'

The curly-haired boy next to him was more philosophical. 'It's crazy the things you forget when you've been here a while.'

Ryan couldn't take it in. 'You mean you never get toilet paper? How do you wipe your butt?'

'You don't,' smirked Three.

'But they have to give us basic essentials. We have rights.'

Three sat up on his bed and looked at Ryan. 'That's where you're wrong, Six. Here, we don't have any rights. They treat us like scum. And you get it even worse. The sooner you appreciate that, the better. Get back against the wall.'

Ryan sighed and returned to his original spot, leaning against the grey bricks.

And you get it even worse.

What did that mean? Everyone here was guilty of something, so why was he going to be treated worse than anyone else?

It didn't make sense.

Ryan waited a few minutes before risking his next question. 'So, is this what you do all day? Hang out in here with nothing to do?'

'We wish,' replied the smallest boy. 'This is the best part of the day. The only time when someone isn't on our case.'

Three cut him off. 'Quiet, Two. He'll find out soon enough.'

'Forget him,' agreed Four. 'Our food's here.'

Everyone jumped off their bunks and stood to attention. Ryan stayed where he was, unsure whether he should follow suit.

There was the sound of a key turning. The steel door creaked open and two guards walked in, the helmets with mirrored visors hiding their faces. One of them held a tray of food, which he placed on the ground. Then he turned to Three.

'You remember the terms of the deal?'

'Sir, yes, sir.'

'Good.'

The soldiers turned and left, slamming the door.

As soon as they'd gone, the cadets descended on the tray, like starving animals.

'Cheeseburgers. I can't remember the last time I had one of these.'

'And they're hot.'

'I'm in heaven.'

'Is that chocolate cake?'

'And there's an extra piece.'

Ryan stepped forward, his stomach rumbling. The last few days, all he'd eaten was hospital food, and the smell made his mouth water.

'Which one's mine?'

'This one.' Three held up a burger and bit into it. 'But

I think me and the lads will eat it, if that's ok with you?'

Ryan pushed forward, sick of being bullied. 'Give it here.'

Four turned on him so fast Ryan was caught off guard. The large lad punched him hard in the stomach, dropping him to the floor.

'Keep away from the food, Six.'

'But I need to eat,' gasped Ryan, surprised at the forcefulness of the attack.

Three gave him a sharp kick, making Ryan groan. 'Not today. Today, you stay hungry.'

Ryan looked up at them, feasting on the burgers. The curly-haired kid had already made a start on his chocolate cake, pure joy in his eyes.

They don't normally eat food this good.

Maybe that's why they were being defensive about it, and why they were stealing his? But why was the food better today than normal?

Suddenly, it clicked into place.

'The governor's making you do this.' He said it quietly, almost to himself, but Three still heard.

'Clever boy.' The blond kid bent down and ruffled Ryan's hair with his greasy hand. 'I wondered how long it would take you to work it out, but we thought it would be a couple of days at least.'

'He's bribing you to make my life hell. That's why we can't be friends.'

'Congratulations.'

'Does he always do that when new prisoners arrive?'

Three shrugged. 'No, just you. But, who cares? We got burgers.'

'And chocolate cake,' said Two, spitting crumbs from his mouth as he forced the last bit in.

'And you're happy about it?' Ryan couldn't suppress his anger. 'You're ok with him using you like that? Letting him manipulate you with cheeseburgers? Do you know how pathetic that is? I thought you guys were tough.'

That hit the mark. Three stopped eating. He narrowed his eyes. 'You know what? I might have felt guilty about what we were doing to you. But now, I'm going to enjoy it.'

Why didn't I keep my mouth shut?

As Ryan tried to clamber to his feet, Three swept his hand away with his foot. 'Stay on the floor, Six. It's where you belong.'

5. POND

When the others had finished eating, the guards reappeared in the doorway. 'Six, come with us.'

Ryan shrugged. 'Whatever.'

The guard whipped the metal baton around and it caught Ryan on the neck, sending an electric shock through his body and knocking him to the ground.

As he cowered on the floor, he saw Three staring at him from across the room, an evil glint in his eye.

'The correct response is *sir, yes, sir*. Do you understand?' The guard lifted the baton again. It hovered near Ryan's face.

'Sir, yes, sir.' He forced out the words, wondering how many times he'd forget their stupid rule.

'On your feet.'

Ryan clambered up, and the guards led him out of the dorm, down the short corridor to the black room with the screen. The silhouette of the governor appeared in front of him. It looked like he was finishing his dinner.

'Ah, Six. I trust you're settling in with your roommates?'

How much should he let on he knew? There didn't seem to be any point hiding it.

'Sir, it would be easier if they hadn't been bribed to torture me, sir.'

Out of the corner of his eye, Ryan saw one guard raise the baton, and waited for the shock, but it never came. The governor found his response amusing rather than impertinent.

'How unfortunate for you. Any idea why I would do that?' From what Ryan could make out, the governor had picked up a napkin and was wiping his mouth.

'Sir, no, sir.'

He had ideas of course. He'd assumed it was the governor's way of breaking in rebellious kids. Make sure their first few days are especially harsh, so they learn to comply. But if that was the case, surely it would have happened to the others as well?

'You upset a friend of mine, Six. You cost him a lot of money. I think you know who I'm talking about.'

Conrad Wolff.

When Ryan had sneaked an antivirus into the Wolff Corporation system, it had ruined the man's plans to make billions from new hardware. Wolff had said he'd get his revenge on Ryan. It seemed he wasn't kidding.

'Wolff was insane. He had it coming.'

Another electric shock. This time, Ryan was expecting it. He grimaced but stayed upright.

'He has asked us to make your stay here especially uncomfortable. And offered us a substantial reward if we do. He wants me to send him regular updates of the special measures we're taking, and some footage of your *activities*.'

Ryan couldn't hide his scorn. 'You're pathetic.'

This time the guard jammed the baton into his side hard and held it there for a few seconds. Ryan yelled in pain as he fell against the wall. The other guard grabbed him by his shirt and pulled him up.

'I can see why he hates you so much. I think I'm going to enjoy this as much as he is. It could be a fun few years.'

A fun few years.

Ryan gulped.

The governor picked up a glass and took a sip from it. 'Your file is fascinating, Ryan. Such a rich history of rebellion, and so many weaknesses to exploit. Even your time at Devonmoor Academy doesn't seem to have tamed that wild attitude of yours. But I will.'

Ryan didn't say anything, but he gave the governor a look of pure hate.

The governor chuckled. 'That's exactly what I'm talking about. Perhaps some time on the pond will give you time to reflect? I hope you don't find it too difficult or boring.'

'It can't be as boring as talking to you.'

He knew it was going to get him another electric shock, and it did.

But it was worth it.

***

It was still light outside, but the sun was low and it was no longer quite so hot.

The guards led Ryan through the maze of chain-link fence. The whole place was grey and brown, stainless steel and dried mud. They reached a large cordoned-off area. In it was the dingiest pond Ryan had ever seen.

28

The water was murky, the surface covered in moss. It smelt like raw sewage. Flies and mosquitoes buzzed around his head as the guards led him forward.

At the edge of the pond, a plank of wood stood upright, reaching into the sky. Ryan wondered if they would tie him to it and leave him there.

Instead, the guard pushed the plank, and it dropped with a splash, lying on the surface of the pond, its far end supported by a small post in the middle.

'Over you go.' The other guard prodded Ryan with the stick, forcing him forwards.

Ryan made his way along the plank. The guard didn't follow, which meant he could walk slowly without the threat of any more electric shocks. That was good because the walkway wasn't that wide.

At the far end, there was nothing but a small metal square that was just big enough to stand on. He stepped on to it.

'Make sure both feet are off the plank,' directed the guard. As soon as Ryan was clear, he lifted up the walkway, leaving Ryan marooned on the tiny island.

The guards turned towards the gate.

'You're leaving me here?' shouted Ryan. 'What if I fall in?'

One guard paused and looked back. 'I wouldn't recommend it.'

He turned away, leaving Ryan alone.

Now, what?

Ryan was standing on a tiny square of metal in the middle of the pond. He couldn't lower himself to sit on it because then his legs would be in the water. The bugs were swarming around his face. He swiped with his arms but it was no use.

He considered swimming, but the water looked putrid. Besides, if the boys in the dorm were to be believed, he'd be wearing the same clothes for weeks. He didn't want to make them smell any worse than they already did, and he definitely didn't want them getting soaked.

What, then?

He just had to wait here, for as long as it took for the guards to come back.

And he had a feeling that was going to be a very long time.

***

It was at least two hours before the men returned.

'Had enough, Six?' shouted one.

Ryan's legs ached, and he wanted to sit down. 'Yeah, you win. I'll be good. Let me out of here.'

'Looks like he still hasn't learned his lesson,' said the other guard. 'I think he needs a while longer.'

'Wait! Don't go!' Ryan called after them, frantic.

'Whenever you speak to us or the governor, you begin and end every sentence with *sir*. Perhaps next time you'll remember.'

'Sir, I'm sorry, sir.' Ryan pleaded with them.

But the men still left.

***

Ryan almost lost his balance. More than once. He was so tired, he could barely think straight, let alone stand.

How long were they going to leave him?

It was dark, and Ryan couldn't see much except the stars, but he could hear the mosquitoes buzzing around his ears and feel them biting his skin.

By the time the men came back, Ryan was desperate. They shone a bright light in his face.

'Well, Six, have you learned your lesson?'

'Sir, yes, sir.' Ryan said it like a marine.

'Much better.' The anonymous guard pushed on the plank. As it hit the surface of the pond, some of the stagnant water splashed on to Ryan's trousers.

'Walk back over.'

Ryan didn't need telling twice, but it was easier said than done, even with the guards shining their light on the narrow bridge. He stumbled, nearly plunging into the putrid water.

That would be the worst. If he fell in now, it would mean his earlier efforts to stay dry had been pointless.

Somehow, he made it across, and followed the guards meekly back to his dorm.

He was shattered. By the time he reached the cell, the others were already asleep. That was a relief; that meant he could slip into his bunk without any trouble.

He could make out the vague shapes of the beds in the darkness, and crept over to the empty one he'd spotted earlier.

Kicking off his shoes, Ryan squeezed into the space making as little noise as possible.

Something was wrong.

There was no mattress.

All he could feel was a rusty wire mesh underneath a blanket. It creaked as it took his weight. That made some boys stir.

Ryan swore under his breath.

'Something the matter, Six?' Three was staring down at him from the top bunk opposite.

'Where's my mattress?' hissed Ryan.

'You don't have one. Not any more. It belongs to me. Turns out these beds are a lot more comfortable when you have two.'

'Give it back.'

'Now, now, Six. You don't want me to wake the others and give you a whipping, do you?'

'I can't sleep like this.'

Three chuckled. 'Stay awake, then. But you're not getting your mattress back. Not now. Not ever. You're lucky I left you a blanket and pillow. Keep whining and you'll lose those.'

Ryan lay there, fuming. He'd been bullied before, but there were limits.

He needed to redress the balance, but he didn't know how.

Right now, there was nothing he could do.

He was outnumbered and outclassed.

And he was in for a rough night.

6. RUCKSACK

'On your feet.'

Ryan jerked awake, the metallic voice cutting through his fevered dreams. His body ached after a night tossing and turning on the wire mesh.

He struggled out of the bunk, standing to attention. Three stood opposite. He caught Ryan's eye and smirked. The little jerk was planning something. Ryan had to get him away from the others. Three was only the same age and size as him: he reckoned he could take him in a fight.

'Outside for morning exercise.'

The boys made their way through the door, the guards close behind. They marched to a large rectangle, about half the size of a football pitch, fences on every side. The ground would have been muddy if it wasn't so dry. Right now, it was all dust and dirt, bumpy and cracked.

One guard handed out black wristbands. Ryan examined his. It was a fitness tracker with two readings: time and distance.

Once all the boys had their bands, the guard turned to face them. 'I want three kilometres in under twenty minutes or you'll be repeating the exercise.'

The second guard approached, carrying a huge army

rucksack. He walked over to Ryan. 'One more thing. You'll be carrying this, courtesy of the governor.'

Ryan took it from him. It was so heavy, he almost couldn't lift it.

'Just to be clear, Six, you still need to make the same time as everyone else.'

How is that fair?

Somehow, he stopped himself saying it out loud. It wasn't meant to be fair. That was the point.

'Sir, yes, sir.' Ryan could see Three grinning. With the boys, the governor and the guards ganging up on him, what chance did he have?

'Begin.' The boys darted off to the far side of the field. Ryan wondered if there was a gap in the fence that would take them on a cross-country course, but as soon as they reached the far side, everyone turned to come back.

Running was boring enough when he'd done it at Devonmoor, and that had been through woodland around a lake. Here, they just did lengths of a muddy rectangle.

The rucksack dug into his shoulders as he ran, the weight holding him back. The other lads had already done three lengths before he finished two.

Sweat poured down his face as he pushed on, forcing one foot in front of the other.

You can do this, Ryan.

He was used to exercise. At Devonmoor Academy, they did loads. And they had even forced Ryan to join the cross-country team. By now, he could run with the best of them.

But not with a heavy pack.

A sudden push from behind sent him toppling over in the dirt. Three ran past, a wicked smile on his face. 'Sorry, Six, didn't see you there.'

Ryan's cheeks burned as he clambered to his feet. That boy was gonna get it. It was just a matter of time.

He checked his fitness band. So far, he'd done just under half the distance but it had taken him twelve minutes. He would never make the target.

Still, he struggled on.

***

'Time's up,' shouted the guard.

The boys stopped running and made their way to the gate, handing in their wristbands as they went. It seemed everyone had made the target.

Everyone except Ryan.

'Two point four kilometres,' observed the guard, as Ryan showed him the band. 'You might as well keep yours on. You need to do it again.'

'Another… three… kilometres?' Ryan panted between each word, wishing he could take off the heavy rucksack.

'Yep, but take your time. There's no rush.'

Ryan looked at him, surprised.

'Of course,' added the guard, 'if you take *too* long, you might miss breakfast.'

Ryan wanted to scream at the man. But that's what the guard wanted. And what the governor wanted. They'd probably get extra cash from Conrad Wolff if they made him cry. He wouldn't give them the satisfaction.

He turned and started jogging, every step strengthening his resolve. He couldn't spend the next four years here.

Heck, he couldn't survive four weeks in a place like this.

If he really thought he would be here for years, he'd have given up already. But Ryan didn't plan on staying here for long.

He was going to find a way to escape.

Whatever it took.

***

'Look who it is,' said Three, as Ryan entered the dorm, swigging a large bottle of water, his shirt drenched with sweat.

On the floor was an empty tray with discarded wrappers.

'Let me guess. You ate my breakfast.' Ryan tried to keep his voice even.

'No need to be like that.' Three jumped down from the upper bunk and walked over to him. 'We felt sorry for you, having to do the run again. So, we kept your breakfast safe.'

Ryan couldn't work out if the blond boy was mocking him. 'Where is it?'

'Right here.' Three reached down the front of his trousers and pulled out a cereal bar with no wrapper. 'It might be a little sweaty, but I guess you're too hungry to care.'

The other boys sniggered. They were loving this. Ryan wanted to punch Three hard in the face but they outnumbered him five to one.

Three held out the bar, but as Ryan went to grab it, he dropped it on the floor. 'Oops.'

Ryan hesitated, unsure whether to bend down to pick it up.

'He's gonna eat it,' said Four. 'I told you he would.'

'Nah. He's not that desperate. Not yet.'

Three was right. Ryan wasn't going to humiliate himself. But if he didn't get any food soon, he might reconsider.

'Let's put bets on how long he lasts before he gobbles that up,' suggested Two. 'My money's on bedtime tonight.'

'Depends whether we let him eat anything else before then,' pointed out Three. 'But if I was him, I wouldn't be holding my breath.'

7. COPY

Ryan's stomach rumbled as the boys were led along a corridor with breeze-block walls and no windows. Whoever designed this place needed to get some joy in their life. But he guessed that was the point. There wasn't meant to be any beauty, any relief from the dismal grey. His eyes studied the walls, checking out the position of every camera. He watched carefully as the guards scanned their pass to open the internal doors.

Every system has a weakness.

That's what Mr Davids had taught him. There might be no computers here, but that didn't mean that Blackfell wasn't a system. And any system could be broken; you just had to find its weakness. Blackfell was no different.

The guard had announced it was time for lessons. Whatever they were like, it had to better than sitting in the stinking dorm.

Ryan expected to be taken to a classroom; an old-fashioned one with single desks and a strict teacher. But the reality was much worse.

They ushered each boy through a separate doorway. When Ryan was pushed through his, he found himself in a small cubicle barely a metre squared. It was like being in an empty cupboard. There was no window, no daylight, just the glare of a white LED fitting in the ceiling above.

The desk was little more than a wide shelf with some papers on it. Below it was a small metal stool and a plastic bucket. There was also a screen on the wall in front of him and a thin slot, like a narrow letterbox.

He pulled out the stool and sat down.

He tried to stay calm. He hated being in cramped spaces. He always had, ever since the car crash when he was younger, when he'd almost been crushed. But the cubicle wasn't that bad. It was claustrophobic, but he could still move.

Breathe, Ryan. It's ok. It's just a room.

The screen flickered into life.

The black outline of the governor's head appeared on the usual blue background. Ryan tried to imagine what the man must look like. He could see bristles on the chin - a short beard.

'Welcome, Number Six. You look tired. I hope that you're not finding your stay too uncomfortable?'

Ryan didn't want to risk another few hours on the pond. 'Sir, no, sir.'

He wondered if the governor knew Three had stolen his mattress. If so, he'd probably given the kid some kind of reward for a stunt like that.

'At Blackfell, all of your lessons will take place in this cubicle, where you cannot be distracted by others. I trust that will not be a problem?'

'Sir, no, sir.' Ryan could feel the walls closing in, as if the space was getting smaller by the second.

'You stay in the cubicle for as long as it takes to

complete today's work,' said the governor. 'The faster you work, the quicker you can return to your dorm.'

Oh, great. Like that's any better.

But even the dorm seemed appealing right now, compared to the tiny prison.

'In front of you are two piles of papers. One pile is full of information. The other is blank. Your job is to copy out everything in the first pile. The layout doesn't have to be exact, but if you make any mistakes, that whole sheet will need to be copied again. When you have finished all the papers, you post them through the slot.'

Ryan picked up the first few sheets from the pile and flicked through them. They were full of simple maths problems. Oddly, they were already complete, the answers filled out.

Maybe it was a test to see if he'd admit to being given the wrong papers, to get him to cheat so they could punish him for it later? He wasn't about to fall for that.

'Sir, these sheets have the answers on them, sir.'

'What's your point, Six?' asked the governor, sounding amused.

'Sir, I won't learn anything from copying these, sir.'

'Like I said, what's your point?'

Ryan didn't know how to answer, but the governor wasn't expecting him to.

'Think about it, Six. We don't want you *learning* anything. Not really. Society is a lot safer if boys like you remain stupid and ignorant. The only lessons you need to learn here are about discipline. But we have certain educational obligations, and this is how we choose to fulfil them.'

Ryan checked out the rest of the pile, struggling to hide his horror at the amount they were expected to copy.

'Sir, you want me to copy all of this *today*, sir.'

'Every word, Six. You'll get another pile tomorrow. And the day after that. Don't forget, there are no weekends here. Every day is the same. Unless you're in solitary or the Pen. Then, it's worse.'

I am in solitary.

Ryan bit back the words. If that was worse than this, he didn't want to know.

'The fastest anyone has finished lessons was in two hours, eleven minutes. The slowest was, well, they may have been in here for days.'

'Sir, but what if I need the toilet, sir?'

Ryan already knew the answer.

'Use the bucket.'

***

His wrist ached.

Copying this amount was hard work. Ryan was bored out of his mind but he had to keep his brain active enough to prevent him from making mistakes.

Some of the answers weren't even correct. Either the governor was trying to mess with his head or he wanted the boys' work to show errors.

Not all the sheets were maths. There were pages about geography too. Facts printed off the internet in the same tiny font.

At Devonmoor, things had been difficult. The

brightest kids in the country were there, and the lessons were intense. Ryan had studied fractal maths and game theory, emotional intelligence and quantum computing. Often, he'd felt out of his depth and sometimes he'd gotten in trouble for it. But at least he'd learned loads. They had stretched him to his intellectual limit. And, if he was honest, he'd enjoyed the challenge.

That wouldn't happen here. There was no hope of learning anything.

At least it's easy.

That's what he tried to tell himself. But it didn't make him feel better. He would spend hours every single day in this stupid cubicle copying things out, and it was all pointless.

Ryan started on the next sheet, wondering which part of Blackfell he was going to hate the most. He still had seven more sheets to go, but there was nothing he could do but press on.

Eventually, he finished the last sheet.

Ryan gave a long sigh and pushed the papers through the slot.

What now?

He looked up at the camera. 'Sir, I'm finished, sir.'

No response.

He checked the door, but it was still locked.

Great. He was stuck in the tiny cubicle with nothing to do. He was so tired, he rested his head on his arms on the desk in front of him.

It wasn't long before he dozed off.

The rustling of paper disturbed him. They had pushed two sheets back through the slot. On the top sheet were three words: 'Copy these again.'

He must have made mistakes. Either that or they were just making him repeat the exercise for the fun of it. He picked up the pen and a blank sheet of paper and got to work, wondering if they would ever let him out of the cramped space.

8. COURT

When Ryan got back to the dorm, the other boys were sitting on their beds, munching sandwiches. He expected they'd have taken his, but one was still on the tray. Next to it was a full bottle of water.

'I get to eat?' he asked.

'Knock yourself out,' sneered Three.

Ryan eyed it suspiciously. 'What did you do to it? Stick it in your pants?'

'You'll never know.' Three took a swig of his drink. 'It might be perfectly fine.'

All the boys watched to see if he would take the sandwich.

He was so hungry. Did it matter if they'd done something to his food?

He crouched down and pulled the slices of bread apart.

Then, he almost threw up.

Along with the thin slice of ham and cheese, the sandwich was full of small curly hairs. He threw it across the room in disgust.

'Hey, don't waste your food,' teased Three. 'The guards are not gonna be happy with you.'

'Screw the guards.' Ryan clenched his fists.

'I think he's angry,' observed Two.

'Hangry more like,' pointed out Four.

'What about the drink? Did you spit in it?'

'You better hope that's all we did.'

'Why don't you taste it and find out,' sniggered Four.

Ryan kicked it, sending it flying.

'I need food.'

'You still haven't eaten your breakfast.' Three held up the cereal bar from earlier and the others laughed.

Ryan's stomach was in knots. He was weak with hunger and in no state to fight. Not with them all in the room.

'If you're not gonna eat anything, you might as well go to your little spot by the wall,' suggested Three.

It was more than a suggestion, and Ryan knew it. He slouched over to the edge of the room and slumped down on the floor.

'Did I say you could sit down?' asked Three.

'Just leave me alone!' shouted Ryan. 'I haven't done anything to you.'

Four lumbered over.

Ryan knew that if he didn't stand, he would get a serious kicking, so he scrambled to his feet. 'Fine, I'm standing. Happy now?'

'We don't want to look at your ugly mug. Face the wall.'

Ryan did as he was told. He could hear the boys sniggering behind him.

He might have avoided another beating, but his self-esteem had still taken a battering. And the humiliation was worse than anything else.

He couldn't let them keep treating him like this.

He had to fight back.

But how?

***

They got a break.

In the middle of the afternoon, the boys were taken outside to the tatty basketball court Ryan had seen when he'd first arrived. There was still no sign of any other teenagers and Ryan wondered if the six lads were the only prisoners there.

He knew it was pointless to ask, so instead he kept close to the fence, trying to stay out of the way of the other boys. Maybe they'd forget about him if he stayed quiet?

For a minute or two, it worked. Four picked up a basketball and dribbled it like a pro before dunking it through the tired hoop.

Three clapped. 'He's still got it!'

'Come on,' said Two, 'let's sort out teams.'

But Three had a glint in his eye. 'I've got a better idea. How about we give basketball a miss today, and play dodgeball instead?'

The other boys didn't seem convinced. 'You serious?'

'We only have one ball,' pointed out Two.

'That's ok. We only have one target.' Three looked over to where Ryan stood next to the fence.

Four grinned. 'Now I get it.'

'Here's how it works,' explained Three, taking the ball from him. 'It's a free-for-all. You can throw or kick the

46

ball as hard as you like. You get one point if it hits him. Three points if you get him in the face.'

'What if he grabs the ball?' asked Two.

'He's not allowed. That's against the rules, and you wouldn't want to break the rules, would you, Six?'

Ryan held up his hands. 'I don't want to play. Why don't you just play basketball?'

'Because,' said Three, with menace, 'this is much more fun.' He drop-kicked the ball hard into Ryan's stomach. 'One point to me.'

The ball rolled back towards the group of boys and Ryan gasped for breath as Two ran forward to boot it. He dodged out of the way, just in time.

'That was close,' jeered Four. 'Let me try.'

By now, Ryan was running down the edge of the court. A chain-link fence prevented him from leaving. The best he could do was get as far away from the ball as possible, which was all part of their game.

The ball smashed into the fence, just above his head. If that hit him, it would hurt.

The lads were chasing him down, wildly kicking the basketball whenever it came near them. Sometimes, they got lucky. Ryan took a blow to the backside and deflected another shot with his forearm, but the ball was being kicked at him with such force, he'd be covered with bruises.

He reached the corner.

Three stood facing him, the ball at his feet.

The only thing Ryan could do was charge through the crowd of boys to get to the other end of the court. He decided to take his chances.

Hurtling towards them, Ryan headed for a small gap between Two and Four.

The boys were surprised; they'd expected him to stay in the corner. But Four had quick reflexes for such a big lad. He held out his foot, tripping Ryan up and sending him sprawling on the tarmac.

Ryan tried to scramble to his feet, his hands grazed, but before he could get upright, the ball smacked him hard in the face.

He reached up to find his nose bleeding.

'That'll be three points to me,' grinned Three. 'You know what? I like this game.'

Ryan wasn't quite so keen.

***

He limped back into the dorm with the other boys, his body aching. They'd chased him around the court for an hour, the ball hurtling towards him like a cannon. He was short on breath and covered in bruises.

They'd only just got back before a guard walked in. Everyone stood to attention, Ryan included. He didn't want to give the staff here any more reasons to punish him.

'This dormitory is a disgrace,' said the guard. 'How did that sandwich end up on the floor?'

Three glanced over to the corner where Ryan had discarded his lunch. 'Sir, Six is responsible, sir.'

The guard turned towards Ryan. 'Is this true?'

Ryan sighed. 'Sir, yes, sir.' He wondered whether he should try to explain why he'd done it, but deep down he knew that would be pointless.

'We have a rule here, Six. You make a mess, you clean it up. Perhaps after you have scrubbed this entire dormitory, you will think twice before doing that again. Wait here.'

The guard disappeared for a few minutes, returning with a large bucket of water and a toothbrush. He handed them to Ryan.

'Get to work.'

9. BUCKET

The next three days dragged.

Every hour was torture. One boring or arduous task led to another. There was nothing to look forward to, no break from the routine.

Ryan hadn't got his mattress back, and was still being mercilessly bullied by Three and the others. He'd finally given in and eaten the cereal bar, much to their amusement. Sometimes, he got food. Often, he didn't. It was never enough, and he was always hungry.

Every night was uncomfortable. Every day was harsh.

He couldn't take it.

But while he was battered and bruised, he hadn't given up hope. He was watching carefully, paying close attention to every detail, looking for a way out.

Every system has a weakness.

He was a hacker. He knew that was true. It might be hard to find the weak point, but even a place like Blackfell would have at least one.

He'd already made some interesting observations. As far as he could work out, the lads in his dorm were the only boys there. There was a second dormitory for the girls, but they never saw each other, except on one occasion when he'd glimpsed them through several layers of chain-link fence. He wondered if Kirsty, another student from Devonmoor Academy, was amongst them. She'd been sent here after experimenting on other students, releasing the Fury.

It didn't matter.

There weren't many prisoners; that was the point. The place was tiny for a prison. And that meant there weren't many guards either.

The mirrored visors made it impossible to see the guards' faces, but back at Devonmoor academy, Dr Torren had taught them how to identify people from the way they walked. That came in useful here. Just from their gait, Ryan could tell that they kept seeing the same four guards.

To compensate for the lack of staff, there were cameras everywhere. Ryan imagined the governor sat in front of a bank of screens, observing everything that happened in his little miserable kingdom.

For now.

Every system has rules.

That was something else Mr Davids had drilled into him, back at the academy. And it wasn't only computer programs that were predictable. So were prisons. If Ryan could anticipate how the guards and the governor would react to something, he might use that to his advantage.

It took him three days to gather the information he needed. All the time, they thought they were breaking him, crushing his spirit, killing his hope.

But his brain was working: generating ideas, calculating probabilities, formulating a plan.

51

By the end of the third day, he knew exactly what he needed to do.

***

It was when he was coming back from an evening run that he summoned up the courage to put his plan into action. He knew it was now or never.

As usual, they had given him a heavy pack to carry, so he was coming back later than anyone else. He needed to have an altercation with the guards, but he couldn't make it too obvious. This had to look natural, nothing more than a moment of frustrated defiance.

He started coughing, dropping to his knees in the corridor. It wouldn't look that suspicious; he'd just run another six kilometres with a heavy pack.

'Get up.' The guards had no time for this. One of them raised his baton.

Ryan ignored it and coughed up phlegm, letting it drop onto the tiled floor.

'You're disgusting, Six,' said the guard. He prodded Ryan with the baton, making him yelp with pain.

'Leave me alone!' yelled Ryan, scrambling to his feet. 'I can't help coughing.'

'You've made a mess of the floor,' pointed out the guard. Because of the visor, Ryan couldn't tell if he was annoyed or just making an observation.

'Have I?' yelled Ryan. 'Well, you know what I think of your stupid floor?' He hacked up more phlegm, spitting it on to the tiles. 'Enjoy cleaning that up, you stupid robots.'

'You shouldn't have done that,' said the guard. He stepped forward and jabbed Ryan in the ribs with his baton, holding it there much longer than normal.

The shock made Ryan yell and step back. 'Sir, I'm sorry, sir,' he said, raising his hands in the air. 'I just lost my temper. It won't happen again, sir.'

'Too right it won't,' said the guard. He turned to his colleague. 'Wait here with him. I'll be back in a minute.'

He wasn't gone long. When he returned, he was holding the plastic bucket and the toothbrush. 'You're going to scrub this corridor clean from wall to wall. You understand me, Six?'

'Sir, yes, sir.'

'We'll be back in an hour, and I expect this corridor to gleam, else you'll be doing the other corridors as well. You understand me, boy?'

'Sir, yes, sir.'

The guards left him to it, knowing that he wouldn't be able to get through any of the doors without a key or a security pass.

At least, that's what they thought.

Ryan tried hard not to grin as he got to work. They'd done exactly what he expected, and what he wanted.

You make a mess at Blackfell, you clean it up. That was one of the rules. And he'd just used it to his advantage.

Because now he was alone in the corridor with a bucket of water.

Ryan scrubbed the floor for ten minutes, his heart thudding as he prepared for the next part of his plan. He needed to get his breath back after the long run he'd just

53

done. He knew that any moment now, he'd be running again.

The governor would be watching, probably even sending the video to Conrad Wolff. But they weren't going to be able to watch for long; in a few minutes, Ryan was going to kill the power.

Ryan had noticed that out here in the corridor there were power points, unlike in the dormitory. He had no way of knowing how many different circuits there were in the building, but Blackfell was small. There was every chance that most of the plugs were in the same one. If he tripped it, they'd all go off.

Without his precious cameras, the governor wouldn't be able to see what was happening. Better still, while the cell doors had old-fashioned turnkey locks, the internal doors in each corridor were all operated by magnets. Without power, they'd swing open. At least, that's what Ryan hoped would happen. If he was really lucky, the locks on the automatic gates might be affected as well, or maybe if he got to the security office he could open the gates from there. It was a long shot, but it was worth it.

If he got caught, of course, he would be punished. Severely. But that wasn't the worst outcome. Ryan knew that what he was about to do was stupidly dangerous. He could die.

Better to be dead than to spend another week in this place.

That's what he told himself, but he wasn't sure if it was true. Still, he took a deep breath, picked up the bucket of water and flung it at the plug socket.

10. NUTS

He jumped back as he did it. He didn't want to be anywhere near the water. The risk of electrocution was way too high.

It was good that the bucket was made of plastic. That helped to minimise the risk. It was also good that his canvas shoes had rubber soles. Still, on a list of stupid ways to get yourself killed, this had to be in the top ten.

No electric shock.

That's a good start, thought Ryan. But then he realised that neither had the power gone off. He stared at the plug point in dismay, wondering how so much water couldn't have had an impact.

It hadn't worked.

And now he was for it.

Just as he could feel the despair welling up inside, he heard a crackle and saw a small spark.

Had it worked?

He'd expected to be plunged into darkness, but maybe the lighting was on a different circuit?

The camera in the corner usually had a small red light under the lens. But now, it didn't.

Something had happened, but was it enough?

There was only one way to find out.

Ryan ran over to the door, carefully jumping the large puddle spreading across the tiles. He pulled the handle and was surprised at how easily it opened.

Now Ryan was excited.

He had a real chance to escape.

He hurtled down the next corridor, past the tiny rooms where they copied out their schoolwork, towards the front of the building.

But he could hear voices; the guards were coming.

He slipped inside one of the study rooms and listened at the door, waiting for the footsteps to pass. It wouldn't take them long to search the building. He needed to get outside before they discovered him.

As soon as it was quiet, he ventured back into the corridor and sprinted towards the exit. But at the last minute, he stopped.

It was no good just rushing outside. He'd find himself trapped in a maze of chain-link fences. Without a key, he'd be caught like a rat in a trap. There must be some kind of staff room around here, or a security control room. That was his best bet. He tried a few doors that he'd never been through before. One was a cleaning closet full of mops and buckets. Another opened into some sort of medical room, with nothing but a bed and a first-aid kit.

The third door was the one he was looking for. It led to a staff changing room. Guard uniforms hung in a storage unit on the wall. Tempting as it was to put one on as a disguise, he didn't have time. He did, however, grab one of the metal batons that stood next to it.

A real weapon at last.

There was a second door in the room. Surely, that led to the staff exit. Ryan was about to push it open when someone pulled it from the other side.

And, finally, he found himself face to face with the governor of Blackfell.

It had to be him. Up until now, Ryan had only ever seen a silhouette, but there was no doubt this was the man who had been behind his torture. There was something about the way he stood, about the well-trimmed beard, about the air of authority he carried. This was a man that liked to be in control.

Ryan wasn't sure who was most surprised. Neither of them had expected to encounter the other. He reacted from instinct, jamming the baton into the governor's ribs and pulling the trigger. The man let out a yell and crumpled to the ground.

'It hurts, doesn't it?' said Ryan. He jabbed the man again, getting way too much satisfaction from watching him writhe on the floor in agony.

'STOP! I order you!' spat the governor.

'I give the orders now,' said Ryan. 'Unless you want to see what it feels like when I jam this into your testicles?'

'No. Please.'

'You're going to help me escape.'

The governor gave him a look of total disdain. 'You can't. There's no way out.'

'You sure about that?' Ryan pushed the baton hard into the man's crotch and pulled the trigger.

The governor screamed.

'Now, put your hands on your head, get on your feet, and show me how I get out of this hell-hole.'

'They'll catch you. The guards will be back any second.'

'And they take orders from you. So you'll tell them to leave me alone. Won't you?' Ryan raised the baton.

'You're insane,' said the governor. 'When they catch you, you'll regret this.'

Ryan smirked. 'We'll see. What's through there?' He pointed towards the next room.

'The control room. Where we watch the cameras. And my office.'

Ryan couldn't take his eyes off the man for a second, in case he tried to fight back. 'Do you have guns?'

'No.'

'You're lying.' Ryan pushed the baton against the governor's mouth. 'Tell me another lie and you're gonna get a new level of toothache. Where are they?'

He could see the fear in the governor's eyes. It felt good to be in charge, to be the one making threats.

The man was wise enough not to call Ryan's bluff. 'In the drawer. Over there.'

'Get face down on the floor,' demanded Ryan. As the man did as he was told, Ryan edged over to the drawer. Inside was a small revolver.

'Is this all there is?' asked Ryan, a little disappointed.

The governor glanced over. 'It's a young offender's institute, not an army base. And don't even pretend you know how to use that.'

'I don't need to pretend. Weapons training is a standard part of the curriculum at Devonmoor. Or didn't you know that, *sir*?' Ryan smirked at his enemy, expertly loading the gun. 'Perhaps a demonstration?' Ryan pointed the gun at the governor's leg.

The governor squirmed on the floor. 'No. Please. Don't shoot me.'

'Then start talking. How do I get out of here?'

'There are some keys hanging up by the door. They open the inner gate. The outer gates are operated electronically.'

'From here? Won't they be open now the power's off?'

'No. They'll be on a different circuit.'

Ryan was aware he was running out of time. The guards could come back at any moment and it would be hard to stay in control then. 'Unlock them. Fast.'

The governor climbed slowly to his feet.

Ryan raised the baton in his left hand. 'Quicker. We need to move.'

'You're taking me with you?'

'You're my insurance,' said Ryan, his voice hard. 'If they try to come after me, you die.'

The governor flipped some switches on the control panel and grabbed the large keyring from a hook on the wall. 'Wolff was right about you. He said you were trouble.'

'Trust me,' said Ryan. 'I'm just getting started.'

He jabbed the governor in the back, another shock making the man's body jerk.

It was partly to hurry things along, but something else was motivating Ryan as well. All the anger from the last four days had built up in him, his frustration bubbling over. He wanted to get his revenge, to cause this man pain. If he was honest, he wanted to kill him.

'You'll never get away with this,' said the governor.

Ryan snorted. 'Wolff said that as well.'

They made their way outside and the governor unlocked the first gate.

'Freeze!'

Ryan glanced behind to see two guards holding vicious looking assault rifles, both aimed in his direction. Clearly, the governor had been lying about the revolver being the only gun.

'If you shoot me, I shoot the governor,' said Ryan, pointing the revolver at the man's head. 'Then we both die. So, if I were you, I'd put down your weapons.'

'Do as he says,' ordered the governor. 'The boy is insane. Who knows what he'll do?'

Too right, thought Ryan.

Even he didn't know what he was capable of.

The men lowered their weapons.

But Ryan had underestimated the governor. The guards had distracted him just long enough for the man to fight back. The governor knocked the revolver from his hand, sending it spinning. Ryan jabbed the baton into the governor's stomach, but it was too late to make a difference.

'Give it up, son. It's over.' The guards were approaching, their guns pointed at Ryan. 'Make one false move and we'll shoot you in the leg.'

Ryan swore.

The governor glanced up at Ryan from where he lay on the floor. 'Oh yes, Six. You can say that again. Your little escape attempt has come to an end. And now it's time to face the consequences.'

11. FIGHT

'Are you scared, Six?'

'No,' lied Ryan.

The governor nodded to one of the guards who promptly jabbed his baton into Ryan's side. Ryan instinctively dropped to his knees.

'How about now?' asked the governor.

'No,' said Ryan, knowing it was pointless, but not wanting to give in.

Another shock. This time for longer. Ryan whimpered in pain, his body still tingling long after the baton was removed.

He knew they'd keep electrocuting him until he caved. And then what? Who knew what the governor would put him through now that Ryan had humiliated him?

The governor sat down in an executive swivel chair. All the cameras were back on, the screens showing every part of the facility. 'We can do this all day,' he pointed out. 'Wouldn't that be fun?'

Ryan glared at him.

'Answer the governor,' ordered the guard.

'Sir, no, sir,' said Ryan, through gritted teeth. He might as well say what they wanted to hear. Otherwise, they would just torture him until he did.

'So, you are scared?'

'Sir, yes, sir.'

'Good. Return this boy to his cell.'

Wait. Was that it?

He'd expected the governor to make him stand for hours on the pond, or have him put in solitary. Why would he just send him back to the dorm?

It didn't make sense.

But as one guard pushed him back along the corridor, the other stayed behind for a brief chat with the governor. When they reached the cell, the second guard caught them up and Ryan found out what the governor had planned.

'Six tried to escape this evening,' said the guard. 'Because of that, none of you will eat tomorrow.'

The boys groaned. Now, they'd hate him even more.

But the guards weren't finished. As they left the cell, one of them dropped their baton on the floor.

'Six used one of these on the staff here today. Therefore, the governor would like you to teach him a lesson about how painful they are.'

With that, the guards slammed the door, leaving the baton behind.

Now Ryan understood.

He was being locked in a room with boys that hated him and they had the perfect way to make him suffer.

Three sauntered over to the baton and picked it up. He looked over at Ryan. 'No food for twenty-four hours, thanks to you. Boys, hold him down.'

***

They jabbed him with the stick for what felt like hours.

He yelled and screamed, but that just made them laugh. The boys chased him around the dorm, taking turns to prod him with it, until just the sound of it made him tremble.

'It's like training a dog,' said Three, swinging the stick towards Ryan as he cowered in the corner. 'Beg, Six. Like a puppy.'

A tear ran down Ryan's face. He knew he was beaten. He couldn't stand being electrocuted again. He'd do anything to prevent that. He crouched down and held his hands up in front of him in a childlike pose.

It was the best entertainment the lads had seen for years. They laughed hysterically as Three warmed to his theme.

'Now roll over,' he ordered Ryan.

Ryan did as he was told.

'I wonder how long they'll let us keep this?' mused Three. 'It's pretty useful.'

Ryan had feared the boys before, knowing they could beat him up. But this was worse. They barely needed a reason to jab him with the stick. It was just too much fun.

For them, at least.

'Lick the bottom of my shoes,' ordered Three, sitting down on one of the lower bunks.

Ryan shuffled forwards on his belly and did as he was told.

The boys were baying like hyenas.

And they wouldn't be the only ones laughing.

The governor would be eating popcorn while he watched this. And so would Conrad Wolff.

The worst part was that his hopes of escape had been dashed. No way would they let him get that far again. They would watch him every minute, every second.

He would spend years in this place, being bullied by these lads.

He might not be able to escape.

But he still needed to fight back.

Or it would never end.

***

The next morning, the guards took the baton away. Ryan was relieved. He'd still get shocked every time he spoke out of turn, but nothing could be as bad as being humiliated by Three.

He hated that kid with a passion.

If I could just get him on his own…

Ryan dreamed of what he'd do if they left them alone together. He'd smash the boy's face in. He'd pay for it later, sure. But it would still be worth it. And maybe Three would think twice about picking on him in the future.

A few days later, Ryan got his opportunity.

He had spent another long, dull morning copying out pages in his cubicle. But, when he got back to the dorm, Three was already in there, alone.

Their eyes met.

Three's face turned white. For the first time since Ryan arrived, the kid was afraid.

The door clanged shut behind Ryan, and he heard the key turn in the lock.

'I know what you're thinking,' said Three, jumping down from the top bunk. 'You want to fight me while the others aren't here. I get it. I would too. But it's not a good idea.'

'Yeah, why's that?' Ryan advanced towards him.

'Because they'll punish us both. You're not allowed to fight here.'

Ryan didn't care. He wasn't going to miss his opportunity. They were the same height, the same build. For once, it would be fair.

He charged, knocking the boy to the floor, then jumped on top of him and punched him hard in the face.

It was surprisingly easy. Three squirmed and struggled under Ryan's knees, but he couldn't get away.

'Please. Stop.' Three spat out the words as blood spurted from his nose.

'You bully me; this is what you get.' Ryan got in a few more punches before the door squeaked open and two guards ran in.

'Get off him.'

'Sure.' Ryan landed one last punch which would give Three the mother of all black eyes, then stood up as the guards grabbed hold of him.

'Fighting is forbidden at Blackfell,' said one guard mechanically.

'But stealing someone's mattress is allowed?' shot back Ryan. He jerked as they prodded him with the metal baton, an electric shock coursing through his body.

'You, on your feet.' The other guard gestured to Three.

'Sir, but I did nothing, sir.' Three held his nose as he scrambled up, blood dripping between his fingers.

'You know the rules. Anyone caught fighting gets taken to the Pen.'

'Sir, please, don't, sir!' Three's face was a picture of horror. Ryan got some satisfaction from seeing the bully looking scared, but it also made him uneasy.

Just how bad was the Pen?

They were led along the corridor and taken outside into the brown and grey wasteland, through the maze of chain-link fence.

'Get in.' The guards pushed them in to a square enclosure.

There was nothing there. Just dirt surrounded by a fence topped with coils of barbed wire.

'What about food?' Ryan shouted after them as they slammed shut the gate and walked away.

No reply.

'Happy now?' Three cradled his nose and leaned against the fence.

Ryan grabbed him by the throat. 'Actually, I'm not sure I've finished. Whose stupid idea is it to put two boys who are caught fighting in the same place?'

'We're being watched,' choked Three. His eyes darted up to the camera in the top corner.

'So? We're always being watched. With any luck, they're listening as well, so they'll hear you scream.'

'Not outside,' muttered Three. 'They only have microphones on the ones indoors.'

'Good to know.' Ryan punched Three hard in the gut. The boy doubled over, dropping to the floor.

'Please, don't make it worse.'

Ryan stood over him. 'So now it's *please*, is it? Now your friends aren't here to save you? You're a dead boy, Three. You're gonna pay for what you did to me.'

'Don't you see? This is what the governor wants.'

'He wants you to get beaten to a pulp? Well, for once we're on the same page.'

'No, you idiot. For us to fight. For me to hate you even more.'

'You were happy enough with the arrangement when it meant you got chocolate cake.'

'It's not like that.'

Ryan grabbed Three by his blond fringe and pulled him up. 'Yeah? You play along with the governor's schemes when it suits you. But now I'm calling the shots, you want me to lay off.'

'Release the boy.' The robotic voice from behind caught Ryan by surprise. He turned to see the guards standing by the gate.

'Whatever.' He let go.

The guards entered the enclosure and grabbed Ryan by the arms.

He no longer cared. 'What happens now? I get my own cage?'

'No, you get these.' Cold metal handcuffs snapped around his wrists, securing his hands behind his back.

'Where are you taking me?'

'Nowhere. You stay here.'

That wasn't good.

'You can't leave me like this.' Ryan's protest landed on deaf ears. The guards locked the gate.

Three looked up at him. 'I tried to warn you.' Clinging on to the fence, the kid pulled himself up. 'Not feeling so confident now, eh?'

Ryan backed up. With his hands cuffed behind him, he had no hope of defending himself. 'So, now you're gonna smash my face in?'

Three narrowed his eyes. 'Give me one good reason why I shouldn't.'

'Won't they handcuff you as well?'

'Maybe. But you know how the governor likes to see you suffer. He might not interfere. So, how about we find out?'

12. ACT

Three grabbed Ryan and held him against the fence. He hissed in his ear. 'Here's what we do. We pretend that I'm getting my revenge. I'll try not to hurt you, but you need to make this look good.'

Ryan was almost too shocked to speak. 'Pretend?'

'Yeah. Act like this hurts.' Three brought his fist up to Ryan's face, catching him on the ear, but he pulled back at the last moment, saving him from the worst of the impact. Ryan screwed up his face, as if in pain, and dropped to his knees.

Three kicked him in the stomach, but barely made contact with his foot. Ryan doubled over as if he was winded, his face in the dirt.

'Now you need to beg.'

'What?' Ryan looked up, confused.

'Beg me to stop. Make it look good.'

Ryan pulled a face, as though he was in tremendous pain. 'Is that enough?'

'Almost. Kiss my shoes.' Three pushed his foot near Ryan's face.

'Seriously?'

'If I was beating you up, I'd make you. It has to look real.'

Ryan pretended to kiss Three's dusty shoe. 'Happy?'

'It'll do.' Three spat on him and gave one last kick, more of a push with his foot that left Ryan sprawled on his side in the dirt. 'The governor needs to think I'm still bullying you.'

Ryan squirmed his torso upright and leaned against the fence. 'So, are we friends now? I thought you hated me.'

'I don't hate you. I don't even know you.'

'Why'd you bully me then?'

'You know why.'

'For burgers and cake. Because you're the governor's little pet.'

Three towered over him. He took a step forward. 'Keep talking like that and I'll smash your face in for real.'

'But it's true.'

Three kicked a cloud of dirt in Ryan's face. 'We've got twenty-four hours together. Want to see just how bad they can be?'

Ryan looked away. Three may have all the power, but he had the moral victory.

Three seemed to realise that as well. He sighed and backed away, slumping down in the corner. 'I understand why you're narked. You're new here. You don't get it. But imagine what it's like when you've been here for months. If the governor tells you to do something, it's not like you have a choice.'

'You always have a choice.'

Three snorted. 'Yeah, do as you're told or spend hours on the pond, or days in the Pen. Or in solitary. Or whatever fresh hell he's dreamed up until you give in.

He breaks us all in the end.'

Ryan hadn't thought about what would happen to the boys if they didn't do what the governor asked. 'He threatened you?'

'What do you think? If we play along, we get nice food. If not...' Three trailed off.

'So, what happens now?'

'Best plan is we act it out. Make it look good. We make sure it's all for show. Well, the beatings at least. You'll have to cope with some of the other stuff.'

'And in return?'

'You don't smash my face in every time you get the chance, so we don't end up back here.' Three slammed his hand against the fence in frustration.

'I guess that's fair.'

'Why does the governor hate you so much, anyway?'

'He doesn't.' Ryan tried to get comfortable on the dirt, but the handcuffs made it impossible. 'Well, maybe he does now. But that's not how it started. He's being paid by someone else. Someone who wants to see me suffer.'

'You must be in a lot of trouble.'

'I'm used to it.' That was true, but even Ryan hadn't been in a situation as hopeless as this. Blackfell was killing him. He turned his attention back to Three. 'How about you? How'd you end up here?'

Three trailed his finger in the dirt. 'My mum married this guy who was a total jerk. He worked in the army and seemed to think I'd signed up too. He kept ordering me around, telling me I'd never amount to nothing.'

Ryan nodded. 'What did you do?'

'He took things way too far. Kept calling me names. Grounded me all the time. Wouldn't let me leave the base. So, I decided to teach him and all his little army buddies a lesson.' Three looked up at Ryan, a glint in his eye. 'I laced the food in the canteen with laxative. Powerful stuff I stole from the medical supplies.'

Ryan raised his eyebrows. 'Did it work?'

'Did it ever. Soldiers were crapping themselves all over the place. The toilets were full, the sinks overflowing. It was carnage. It took them days to recover and clean it up. The place still stinks.'

'How'd they find out it was you?'

'Caught on camera.' Three wiped his bleeding nose with the back of his hand. 'I tried to hack the system and wipe the footage, but they traced it back to me.'

'You're a hacker?' Ryan couldn't hide his surprise.

'Most of us are, here at Blackfell. Hackers or terrorists or kids who the government doesn't want to exist. Apparently, the fact that I could hack into the secure system made me a threat to national security. It wasn't the first time I'd screwed up, so they sent me here. My stepdad was glad to see the back of me.'

'How long you in for?' asked Ryan.

'Who knows? They never tell you. That's part of the punishment. I guess if you behave yourself, they let you out sooner than if you don't. But I've been here for months already and there's no talk of release. I don't think my stepdad wants me back.'

'You reckon there's any other way out?'

'No chance.' Three looked up at the barbed wire high above them. 'This place is locked down. No-one escapes. Ever.'

That wasn't what Ryan wanted to hear.

***

It was hours later when the guards came back with some food. It wasn't much, just a couple of bread rolls on a paper plate and two bottles of water.

But with the boys in his dorm constantly eating or sabotaging with his food, Ryan was always hungry. He struggled to his feet.

'Do you think you'll be able to control your temper now?' the guard asked him. Ryan could see his own reflection in the man's helmet.

'Sir, yes, sir.'

'Turn around.'

Ryan twisted away from the guard, allowing him to release the handcuffs.

'If you touch the other boy, these go straight back on,' warned the guard.

But he can do what he likes?

Ryan didn't bother to say it. There was no point.

'You'll need these.' This came from the other guard. He threw down a green sleeping bag and roll mat between the two boys, then the guards turned and left.

Ryan rubbed his wrists and glanced up at Three. 'I don't want to risk another fight. Not if it means I'll end up back in handcuffs. And I need to eat.'

'Ok, stay there.' Three headed over to the food. He grabbed one of the rolls and bottles of water. Then he kicked the remaining roll off the plate and ground it into the dirt with his foot. 'This way, they'll think I'm still bullying you.'

'But I have to eat that.'

'It's just dirt. If I was torturing you for real, I'd have done something worse.' Three returned to his corner to eat his dinner.

It's just dirt.

Three was right. Ryan brushed the worst off the roll and crammed it in his mouth; he couldn't get it into his stomach fast enough.

'I'm guessing we're going to sleep out here,' he said, nodding towards the sleeping bag.

'For sure. Let's hope it's just for one night.' Three sounded serious, like he'd been here before.

'Are we meant to share it?'

'No, we're meant to fight over it. Or you're meant to sleep without one. Who knows? They're probably taking bets.'

Ryan was tired, even though it was only just getting dark. 'So, what *are* we gonna do?'

Three shrugged. 'If I let you use that, it's gonna give the game away. You're just gonna have to suck it up and sleep on the ground.'

'That's what I was afraid of.'

13. TREES

The ground was hard and cold. It was lucky it was June; Ryan didn't want to think about what it would be like to be in the Pen in the winter. He sat up, leaning against the fence, hugging his legs.

It was pitch black now, just a few dim lights visible in the distance. He could make out the dark shape of Three by the fence opposite, curled up in the sleeping bag, sound asleep.

Some of his punishments at Devonmoor Academy had been grim, and there were times when Ryan had been bored out of his mind. But at Devonmoor, life was generally good. He had friends and things to look forward to.

Here, everything was grey and bleak.

He'd been here for less than a week and all joy had vanished from his life, leaving nothing but a pit of despair.

There was no way out.

Don't think about it.

That was the only way he would survive: by focusing on the moment. If he allowed himself to dwell on the fact he might spend years in this place, he'd lose his mind.

A low humming sound interrupted his thoughts. Ryan brushed away a tear and looked around.

Where was it coming from?

At first, he thought it could be an insect, but it was more like a machine or a distant plane.

And it was coming closer.

He stood up and peered into the sky, his eyes searching the blackness.

The hum got louder and Three stirred. 'What is that?'

Ryan was frozen to the spot. 'I think it's an aircraft.'

'Here?' Three sat up, suddenly awake.

As Ryan watched, a dark shape blacked out the stars. He could make out a saucer shape, like a UFO. It was descending towards the Pen.

'It's landing here,' he muttered.

'At Blackfell?'

'No. Right HERE!' Ryan dragged Three back to the fence.

Seconds later, the craft lowered itself to the ground in the middle of the Pen. It was so close, Ryan could almost touch it.

He'd never seen anything like it before, even at Devonmoor. An empty metal chair hung beneath a dark black saucer, which must have been at least two meters across. Above that were four rotors.

'Is it some kind of helicopter?' asked Three.

Ryan frowned. 'It's a giant drone.'

'Are we meant to get in? Is this a rescue?'

'I hope so.'

The sound of movement from the main building jolted Ryan into action. Guards were yelling. Thankfully, they had several gates to unlock before they would make it to the Pen.

'It's now or never,' pointed out Three.

'Let's do this,' agreed Ryan. Whatever happened, it was worth a try.

He dashed forwards and jumped on the chair. Three wasn't far behind, dropping on to Ryan's lap. Seconds later, the craft lifted off. Ryan hugged Three around the waist so he wouldn't fall.

He glanced down to see guards reach the gate of the Pen, floodlights pointed towards the sky. But Ryan and Three were already swooping over the barbed wire and then over the high steel fence that marked the boundary of Blackfell.

Wind rushed around Ryan's ears as the aircraft sped along. He wondered if he was dreaming, but the smell from Three's armpit was too intense. This had to be real.

Three let out a whoop of delight. 'This is wild!'

He was right, but Ryan didn't feel all that safe in the chair. Whoever designed this thing should have at least fitted a seatbelt.

In the darkness, it was hard to make out the landscape below. There was a glistening of stars reflected in a river. The vague silhouette of dark hills. And then something brushed past his leg.

'What was that?' asked Ryan. 'Did you feel it?'

'Yeah, something.' Three squirmed around, glancing down. 'I think it was a tree.'

'We shouldn't be flying that low.' Ryan tried to pull his legs higher, but it was impossible with Three on his lap. 'If our legs get caught in any branches, we'll get pulled out of the chair.'

And our legs will be snapped off and then we'll fall to

our deaths.

He didn't add that last part, but knew it was true.

'You worry too much. We'll be fine.' But as they brushed past a few more trees, Three didn't sound so sure. 'It's losing power.'

The drone was struggling to stay in the air. One rotor stopped, and the vehicle dropped. Three shielded his face from the onslaught of leaves and branches.

Ryan squeezed his eyes shut. This was not going to end well.

Impact.

The drone must have hit a large branch that sent it spinning off course. Both boys went flying. Three screamed.

Ryan smacked into the branch of a tree and tried to grab hold. He slid some way down then hung there, his heart thudding a thousand beats a minute.

A piece of the drone flew past his ear and hit the ground below. The vehicle itself collided with a tree trunk a short distance away. For a while the rotors continued to turn as it tried to break free, but then there was silence.

Except for a groaning some distance away.

'Three?' Ryan could feel himself losing his grip on the branch. He wasn't sure how high up he was, but he knew that letting go would be a really bad idea.

Another groan. 'That hurt.'

'Are you on the ground?'

Three swore. 'Where else would I be?' Then a moment of realisation. 'You're not stuck in the tree?'

'Afraid so.' Ryan barely had the energy to speak and

hold on. He edged along the branch, hoping he could climb down. 'How far did you fall?'

'Hard to tell. I was lucky though. Landed in a bush. But I've hurt my ankle.'

Ryan could just about make out the outline of a sturdy branch below that he could stand on. He let out a sigh of relief as it took his weight. 'I'm not sure if I can climb down.'

'From what I can see, these are high trees. You'd have to drop the last five metres. I wouldn't recommend it.'

'Fine, I'll just live up here then, shall I?' snapped Ryan.

Three went quiet for a moment. Ryan wondered if he'd offended him, but when he spoke again, he sounded thoughtful rather than annoyed. 'You're next to some water. If you can get to the other side of the tree, you might drop into that.'

'Great.' Ryan found it hard to sound enthusiastic about the prospect of dropping into a freezing lake in the middle of the night. But Three had a point. It might be his only way down.

He shuffled further along the branch, towards the trunk. He was glad he couldn't see the ground below. That wouldn't help his concentration. Instead, he peered into the darkness, trying to make out the other branches.

Ryan had spent most of his childhood gaming, not climbing trees, and he clung on for dear life as he shifted his weight from one branch to another. There was a heart-stopping moment where he had to let go of the branch he was holding in order to grasp the next. With some desperate scrabbling, he made it.

'Are you ok?' Three sounded concerned.

'Just about.'

As Ryan edged along, he could see that Three had been right; there was a pond underneath him. But there was no telling how deep it was. Ryan had watched a film once about a kid who had been paralysed by jumping into shallow water. He tried to push it from his mind.

He pulled himself inch by inch along the branch, as far as he dared go, then looked at the glistening surface. It was a long way down.

'I'm over the pond now. I'm about to drop.'

'Sounds like a plan.' Three's voice was still strained. He was in a lot of pain. 'Good luck.'

'Three, if I die, there's something I want you to know.'

'Yeah, what's that?'

'You've been a total pain in the ass.'

Three snorted a laugh. 'If it helps, I'm probably gonna die out here, anyway. I can't walk far, that's for sure.'

'In that case, I'll see you in hell.'

Ryan took a deep breath and let go.

14. SPLASH

Time stood still.

Ryan fell into the blackness, his heart in his throat.

When he hit the murky water, it was an anti-climax. He splashed down, dragging pond algae under the surface as he went, bending his legs in case the water was shallow. He needn't have feared. Wherever the bottom was, he never touched it.

Ryan wasn't the strongest swimmer, but he knew the basics. Pure desperation got him back to the surface where he spat out a mouthful of foul-tasting water.

He could hear Three calling. 'Six? You there?'

'Yeah,' gasped Ryan, using the last of his energy to push his body to the edge of the pond and drag himself on to the mud. 'You don't get rid of me that easily.' He lay there shivering and exhausted.

'You need to keep moving,' said Three, limping towards him. 'Else you'll freeze to death.'

Ryan knew Three was right, but he was so tired. His body just needed a few moments to recover. A minute or two wouldn't hurt.

The wood was peaceful, and he could relax.

Three was saying something else, but Ryan couldn't focus.

Right now, he just needed to sleep.

***

'Six! SIX!'

Three was shaking him violently.

'What? What is it?'

'You're gonna die if you stay there.'

Ryan felt a weird sensation in his legs. Three had pulled off his trousers.

He looked up, confused. 'What the hell are you doing?'

'You'll get hypothermia. Take your top off. And your boxers. Quick.'

'But it's freezing!'

'That's why you have to get out of those wet clothes.'

Ryan reluctantly pulled off his t-shirt. 'You sure you don't just want to get me naked? This is the second time you've made me strip.'

That made Three smile. 'Don't flatter yourself. I'm not into boys. And if I was, I don't think your scrawny body would do the trick. Here.' Three tugged off his camo shirt and handed it to Ryan. 'Put this on. You need it more than I do.'

Three was right. The moment Ryan pulled on the dry shirt, he felt a million times warmer.

'What about my legs?' he asked.

To Ryan's surprise, Three took off his own trousers and handed them to Ryan. 'These were yours anyway. Did you lose your shoes in the pond?'

'I had to kick them off to swim.'

'Better keep your socks on then, for protection. Just

83

wring them out.'

Ryan did as he was told, squeezing the water out of the thick boot socks before pulling them back on. He felt a lot better now he was on the ground in mostly dry clothes. Three stood nearby, just visible in the moonlight. Now he'd donated some of his clothes to Ryan, he was only wearing a t-shirt, boxers and socks. But at least he still had his shoes.

'Now what?' asked Ryan.

'We get going. They might know where we crashed. It won't be long before they come after us. We need to keep moving.'

'Which way?'

'Your guess is as good as mine. Any idea which direction we came from?'

Ryan shook his head. After the drone collided with a tree, it had spun out of control. 'So, let's get this straight. We could end up walking right back to Blackfell?'

'Maybe,' admitted Three. 'But if we get out of these woods, we might get our bearings. And if we stay here, we're bound to get caught. So, let's just pick a direction and walk.'

'Fine by me.'

Three looked uneasy. 'Thing is, Six, I might need some help. My ankle's pretty messed up.'

'I'll do you a deal,' said Ryan.

'What's that?'

'I'll help you walk, if you stop calling me Six. My name's Ryan.'

Three snorted. 'Sure thing, *Ryan*.'

'That's better.' Ryan put his arm around Three's

shoulder and they took a few tentative steps forward. 'Does that help?'

'A little. I think you need to be the other side.'

It took some practice, but the boys worked out a way they could limp along, arm in arm, through the undergrowth. With Three's swollen ankle and Ryan having no shoes, it was slow going.

Three was in a lot of pain. Ryan wasn't sure how far they could go. He didn't want to admit it but their chances of escape weren't good. The drone had arrived unexpectedly, and they had no plan.

'When we get out of the woods, what then?' panted Ryan, after a while.

'I don't know, do I?' snapped Three. 'We have to figure this out as we go. One thing's for sure: we can't let them take us back to Blackfell. I don't even want to know what the governor will do to us. I'd rather die.'

Ryan felt the same.

'I still don't know your name,' he pointed out. 'I can't keep calling you Three.'

'Yes, you can. I prefer it to my name.'

'Yeah? What's that?'

'I'm not saying.'

They walked for over an hour, stopping for an occasional rest. The woods looked the same here as they did where they had crashed. It felt like they hadn't moved at all.

The only thing that had changed was the sky: it was getting lighter; the first hints of dawn.

Three stiffened. 'Wait? Do you hear that?'

Ryan listened. There was a distant buzzing sound.

'Is that another drone?'

'Come to rescue us, maybe?' said Three.

'Or the governor sent it to find us,' pointed out Ryan. 'It doesn't sound as big as the last one.'

Three looked around. 'We have to hide. Just in case.' He tugged Ryan towards a fallen tree. 'This'll do. Get as far under as you can.'

The boys dropped to the floor and tucked their bodies out of sight. The tree trunk wouldn't cover them completely, but from the right angle, it might prevent them from being seen.

The stench of wet, rotting wood filled Ryan's nostrils. Something crawled up his leg, and he tried to shake it out.

As they lay there in the dirt, the buzzing got louder and louder, until it was overhead. Then, it carried on, disappearing into the distance.

'Do you think it saw us?' muttered Three, dragging himself out.

'No, I think it would have paused.' Ryan helped the blond boy to his feet. 'But who knows how long it'll be before it comes back. We better keep moving.'

Three hesitated, then gave Ryan a strange look. 'Can I ask you something? And I want you to be honest.'

'Sure. Whatever.'

'We're screwed, aren't we?'

'Totally. Our chances of pulling off an escape are like one in a million. And we don't have anywhere to go.'

'But someone tried to rescue us,' pointed out Three. 'Maybe they have a plan?'

'I sure hope so.'

As they started limping along, Ryan thought about Three's words. He was right. Someone had sent a drone to save them.

But something had gone very wrong with the rescue. And time was running out.

15. TENTS

After another hour of hiking through the undergrowth, the boys were struggling. Ryan's feet were sore and Three still couldn't put any weight on his ankle.

The little hope they had was fading away.

'Is that a road?' asked Three.

They limped as fast as they could towards it.

It was a road. But there wasn't a vehicle in sight.

'You thinking we should hitch-hike?' asked Three. 'We can't walk much further.'

'We could try. But people might be on the lookout for us and report us.'

'So, we stay off the road?'

Ryan frowned. 'Roads lead to places. We could walk for miles through woods and moors, even go in circles if we're not careful. I think we follow the road and hope no-one sees us. At least while it's quiet.'

'It'll be easier to walk on tarmac,' added Three. 'I think there's a sign down there.'

Ryan peered into the distance. 'Wait here. I'll go and check what it says.'

'Suits me. I could use a rest.' Three slumped down by a tree while Ryan padded down the side of the road in his damp socks.

It only took him a few minutes to get close enough to

make out the words: 'Campsite. 500 yards.'

Despite his tiredness, Ryan almost ran back to Three. 'It's a campsite. Really close.'

'And?' Three couldn't see why Ryan was excited. 'Surely that's a place we should avoid?'

Ryan leaned against a tree while he caught his breath. 'No. Think about it. It's easy to break into tents, even if they're locked. People will have plenty of food and drink, and we might bandage your foot. And find you some trousers. And get me some shoes.'

Three grinned. 'What we waiting for?'

The lads set off with renewed enthusiasm. It didn't take long to cover the five hundred yards. As they approached the main entrance, they veered off the road so they could sneak in from the woods.

It was a scenic campsite, with pitches in small clearings between the trees. A neat wooden cabin at the far end was signposted as a toilet and shower block. The thought of taking a hot shower made Ryan want to cry. Would they be able to get clean at last?

A short chicken-wire fence was all that marked the edge of the site, and the boys hunkered down behind a bush, keeping watch.

'Here's how this works,' said Ryan. 'We watch from a distance, wait for someone to head out for the day. Then, we sneak into their tent.'

Three looked impressed. 'I'm game.'

In the clearing in front of them were three tents. One was an orange frame tent that must have been at least twenty years old. Another was a top-of-the-range dome tent with three sleeping compartments. The third tent was blue and shaped like a tunnel.

The first sign of movement came from the orange tent. A man in his seventies unzipped the door and stepped out. He was wearing corduroy shorts and a vest.

'Hey, Three,' muttered Ryan. 'I reckon those clothes would suit you.'

Three punched him on the arm. 'I think they're more your style.'

The old man sat down in a deck-chair and fired up the gas burner to boil a kettle.

Ryan had known that his plan would take a while to enact, but as he watched the man potter about making tea, he realised just how long it was going to be before anyone left the campsite. 'Might as well get comfortable. I think we're in for a long wait.'

Three yawned and lay back on the dirt. 'I can live with that. Wake me up when it's showtime.'

The kettle whistled and the old man started pouring his tea.

Ryan gritted his teeth as he watched. He was tired and hungry and desperate for food. But he could tell there wouldn't be much to be excited about in that man's possessions. Hopefully, there would be a better tent they could break into.

He was right.

There was.

Twenty minutes later, Ryan smiled as a teenager stumbled out from the large dome tent and set off to the toilets. The boy couldn't be far off fourteen. His sister followed; she was a few years younger.

Before they'd returned, the parents had begun cooking breakfast, the smell of bacon wafting towards the boys' hiding place.

Ryan tried to ignore it, but his stomach rumbled in protest. He'd hardly eaten for days. He'd kill for a piece of bacon right now.

It was torture watching the family eat. They looked so relaxed and content. It reminded Ryan of holidays with his own family, of everything he'd lost.

I have to get my life back.

No way was he going to spend the rest of his days on the run, terrified of being caught and dragged back to Blackfell. There had to be a way to clear his name.

Later, Ryan. Focus on the present.

After the breakfast came the washing up. Everything took so long: fetching the water, heating it on a stove, rinsing the dishes. Even the old couple in the tent opposite had finished their breakfast and headed out on a walk before the family were done.

Come on!

Eventually, the family seemed to stir themselves into action, grabbing some bags and heading towards the small car park at the other end of the site.

Ryan nudged Three. 'It's time.'

The blond boy sat up and rubbed his eyes. 'Yeah? Which one?'

'The blue dome tent. They have a teenage boy. His stuff should fit us. And I reckon they'll have a ton of food in there.'

'So, what you waiting for?'

'I have to do this?'

'I can't go down there like this.' Three gestured to his injured foot and his underwear. He had a point.

'Fine. Keep a lookout.'

Ryan crept forward, double-checking there was no-one around. He pulled himself over the chicken-wire fence, snagging the baggy camo trousers. He couldn't wait to get his hands on some normal clothes.

Still, a boy wearing combats wasn't too unusual, even in a place like this. He walked towards the tent as if he owned it, then crouched down to unzip it.

They hadn't locked the outer compartment, which meant he had easy access. That's where all the food and drink were stored.

The sight of it almost sent Ryan over the edge. He couldn't wait a second longer. He snatched a bottle of water and twisted the lid off, gulping down the contents as fast as he dared. Ripping open a packet of biscuits, he crammed them into his mouth, desperate for sugar.

There was an entire bag full of food; he'd haul that out when he left so he and Three could have a feast. But first, he had to see if he could get hold of some clothes. Still munching on biscuits, Ryan crouched down to inspect the inner tents. These were padlocked shut, the two zips on each door secured together.

Ryan didn't understand why. It was a tent; it was hardly difficult to break into. He snatched a kitchen knife from the pile of cooking equipment and cut a long line into the door so he could step through, cursing as he saw the bright pink sleeping bag and a suitcase full of girls' clothes.

The next compartment was the one he was after. A

gym bag overflowed with jeans and hoodies. He stuffed the clothes back inside it, before zipping it up and hauling it out.

And then he saw the jackpot: a spare pair of trainers. Only one size too big. Ryan stuffed his feet into them, relieved to have some shoes at last.

Should he check the parents' compartment too? Probably. He sliced a hole and rooted through the suitcase in there, but there was no point. There was nothing worth taking; the family had taken all their cash and valuables with them.

Wise people, thought Ryan.

Still, it was going to be a shock for them when they got back to find their tent wrecked and their stuff gone.

He didn't feel guilty. They looked like a family who could afford it.

He rummaged through the food and drink, stuffing a supermarket bag full of the best stuff, then headed for the door, pleased with his haul.

But just as he was about to unzip it, he heard something that made his blood freeze.

Voices.

And they were coming this way.

16. CLEAN

'I'll put the kettle on.'

It was the old man and his wife.

At least it wasn't the family coming back. No-one was about to step into the tent and discover Ryan stealing their supplies.

But the couple might have got to know them, camping so close. If so, they'd know that Ryan wasn't part of the family and shouldn't be in the tent. He couldn't just walk out with two bags of stuff.

Ryan could hear water being poured into a kettle, and then a gas burner being lit. He'd already seen how long it took the old man to make tea.

Should he wait in here while they drank it?

What if the family returned?

Besides, even afterwards, the couple might hang around for ages. They might never leave.

What then?

Ryan quietly unzipped the gym bag and rummaged around. He could change into some of the boys' clothes, pulling on a hoodie to hide most of his face. Then he could try to slip past them to the shower block. But it was a high-risk strategy. What if the couple wanted to talk? What if they wondered where the rest of the family were?

Think, Ryan, think.

As he looked around, the answer came to him.

He could go out the back of the tent.

There was no door, but that didn't matter; he could make one. Taking the knife, he made one last cut between two of the sleeping compartments, allowing him to escape, out of sight of the old couple. He hauled the bags out and stole over to the chicken-wire fence.

When Ryan reached the hiding place, Three looked surprised.

'How did you get past the old duffers?' he asked.

Ryan smiled. 'I have my methods.'

'Ok, Houdini. I thought you were a gonner.'

They spent the next half hour behind the bush, stuffing themselves with food and guzzling drink. They were so hungry, they almost finished it all, but Ryan didn't care. They needed energy more than they needed supplies.

Three let out a small burp and lay back on the ground. 'That was *so good.*'

'We should get changed,' pointed out Ryan, pulling the gym bag towards him. 'But I'm wondering whether to risk a shower.'

'You serious?' Three propped himself up on his elbows. 'You think it's worth it?'

Ryan nodded. 'We could freshen up and no-one would know. There's nobody about. Besides, we need to get your wound cleaned out. It looks nasty.'

'True.' Three glanced over at the shower block. 'If we edge around the campsite, we wouldn't have to walk far to the showers.'

'Come on,' said Ryan, standing up. 'Let's do it.'

The boys made their way around the perimeter of the campsite, then jumped the fence, Ryan carrying the gym bag.

A few kids were playing frisbee some distance away, but didn't pay them any attention.

The boys were relieved to find the shower block was empty. The cubicles were open, ready to use.

Three dashed into one of them and Ryan took the one next to it. Slamming the doors shut, they stripped off as fast as they could.

Ryan dumped the army gear on the floor. He couldn't care less about the fact it would get wet. He wasn't going to wear it again.

The water was only lukewarm, but compared to the conditions at Blackfell, it was five-star luxury. There was some shower gel in the bag, and Ryan smothered himself with it before throwing it over the partition to Three. 'No offence, but you need some of this.'

Three laughed. 'I think I'm in heaven.'

Ryan had only been in Blackfell for a week. He couldn't imagine what it would be like to have a warm shower after you'd been there for months.

After way longer than was necessary, Ryan turned off the water and dried himself with a beach towel he'd found in the bag. Then he rummaged around for something to wear.

'Any chance of a towel?' asked Three.

'Use this.' Ryan threw over the towel he'd just used. 'I'll find us some clothes.'

He pulled on some clean underwear and then tried

on some football shorts. They were too big but he could tie the cord to stop them falling down. He slipped on a navy-blue polo shirt and popped up the collar, feeling like a real teenager for the first time in months.

After he'd grabbed some white socks from the bag, he stuffed the army clothes in with the other stuff and zipped it back up. 'I'll pass over the bag so you can find yourself some stuff to wear.'

'Sounds good.'

Ryan flung the bag over the wall and heard Three catch it on the other side. Then he jammed his feet into the trainers, opened the cubicle door and made his way over to the sink. He looked tired, sure. And a bit beaten up. But he felt great. For the first time in forever, he was clean. And he was free.

Three emerged, wearing cargo shorts and a rainbow tie-die t-shirt, his face shining. 'I found this in the bag.' It was a comb, but he looked like a boy who hadn't seen one in years.

'I need that after you,' said Ryan.

'You sure do.' Three ran it through his hair for what felt like an age.

'You finished?' asked Ryan.

'I guess. Believe it or not, I used to have a decent hairstyle, before Blackfell.'

'Sure you did,' teased Ryan. He grabbed the comb from Three and dragged it through his own hair. 'How's your ankle?'

'It stung like crazy, but now it's clean, it looks a lot better.' Three pulled down his sock to show Ryan the wound. It was a deep gash, but it had stopped bleeding.

'We should get out of here. The family will be back soon and all hell will break loose.'

'What do we do with the bag?' asked Three.

'Leave it here. It'll only slow us down.'

'There's just one more thing I need.' Three stuck his hand in the bag and felt around. He pulled out a pair of sunglasses and slipped them on. 'How do I look?'

'Like a rock star,' grinned Ryan. 'At least they hide the black eye.'

Three was still limping as they made their way outside. He tripped and bumped into a man who was entering the shower block.

'Sorry,' he muttered, embarrassed.

'No harm done,' said the man, pushing past.

Once they were outside, Three started limping more quickly, heading towards the car park.

'Hey, what's the hurry?' asked Ryan.

Three spoke quietly, careful not to be overheard. 'We need to steal a car.'

Ryan couldn't hide his shock. 'Are you insane?'

'No, I've thought about it. As soon as that family come back, they'll report the theft to the police. We have to be as far away as possible by then.'

'Can you even drive?'

'Sure. It's easy. I used to joy-ride in my stepdad's BMW.'

'But they'll be able to trace us.'

'Once we get to a town, we dump it,' explained Three. 'It'll be much easier to hide amongst other people. Out here, they'll soon find us if they scan the area with drones. We can only hide for so long. Our body heat will give us away.'

Ryan didn't want to admit it, but Three had a point. Nevertheless, stealing a car wouldn't be easy. 'Let's say you're right. How do we do that?'

'I thought you'd never ask.' Three reached into his pocket and pulled out some car keys. 'Come on, it won't take that guy long to discover these are missing.'

Ryan could see how Three had ended up in Blackfell. 'How do we even know which car is his?'

'Like this.' Three pressed the button on the keyring. The lights flashed on a dark grey hatchback, and they could hear it unlock. 'Am I a genius or what?'

Ryan wasn't sure that was the word he'd use. Three had taken a colossal risk, stealing the keys. Just because he'd gotten away with it, didn't make it a good idea. 'You're crazy, that's for sure.'

Three dropped into the driver's seat. 'You coming or not?'

17. GETAWAY

Ryan hesitated.

'Come on,' urged Three. 'We can't hang around.'

He was right. Ryan opened the car door and took a deep breath.

Three sounded angry now. 'Hurry! What's your problem? Do you *want* to get caught?'

'It's just…' Ryan slipped into the passenger seat, his hands shaking as he fumbled for the seatbelt.

'Just what?' Three turned the key and revved the engine before Ryan had even closed the door.

They heard an angry shout. A short distance away, they could see the man they'd bumped into in the shower block running towards them.

'Looks like someone's on to us.'

Three looked over his shoulder as he slammed the car into reverse. The vehicle shot back. There was the crunch of metal and broken glass as it collided with another parked car.

Three didn't even seem to notice. He changed gear, and with the mother of all wheelspins, they zoomed forwards, out of the car park and away from the angry camper. He gave the man a rude hand gesture out of the back window.

'Hey, leave the guy alone,' said Ryan. 'I'd be mad if

you'd just stolen my car.'

'We need it more than he does.' Three swerved on to the main road and floored the accelerator.

Ryan opened his window, desperate for fresh air.

'You get travel sick?' asked Three. 'You're white as a sheet.'

'Something like that.' Ryan grimaced. 'I was in a car accident a few years back. It was bad.'

Three swore. 'No wonder you're nervous. So, you hate being in a car now?'

Only with you at the wheel.

Ryan didn't say it because he didn't want to offend Three, but the way the kid was driving, it was only a matter of time before they flew off the road and collided with a tree.

Then it would be just like last time.

He tried not to think about the accident. The way the flames burned while he choked on the smoke. Sharp metal pinning his body to the seat.

He wanted to get out, but they had to get as far away from the campsite as possible before they abandoned the car.

'Are you ok?' Three took a corner way too fast.

Ryan's voice was strained. 'Can you just concentrate on what you're doing?'

'Hey, don't sweat it.'

'I thought you said you'd driven before?'

'I did. But it didn't end so well.'

It took a moment for the words to register. Then Ryan realised what he'd said. 'You crashed?'

'Yeah. Total write off. My stepdad was not a happy

man.' Three grinned as though he'd told a joke. 'He deserved it though.'

Somehow, knowing that made the whole thing worse. Three seemed to think he was invincible and that crashing a car was no big deal. Ryan knew different after his own experience; he'd nearly died and spent months in hospital.

'Do you think we can slow down?' he asked.

'Not a good idea. That man's gonna have reported us to the police. They take joyriding seriously. We don't have long before they trace us.'

'Then I say we dump the car and run.'

'Soon,' agreed Three. 'Look.' He nodded to a sign up ahead. 'It's only two miles to Shetford wherever that is. If they have a train station, we can bunk a ride out of here.'

They hadn't driven past many cars, but as they approached the town, Ryan slumped down in his seat as he saw a police car coming from the opposite direction.

Three let off a string of swear words. He slowed down and sat up in the seat, pushing the sunglasses up his nose. He was trying to look like he was just an innocent driver minding his own business.

As they passed the police car, though, Ryan could see the suspicious look on the officer's face. Sure enough, as soon as it had passed them, the car slowed to turn around.

'We're busted. We need to get out of here.'

Three slammed on the accelerator and they shot forward. The trees gave way to the outskirts of a town.

A petrol station. Houses. They could hear sirens.

'This was a stupid idea,' said Ryan. 'We'd have stood a better chance walking.'

Three was so focused on what he was doing, he didn't even try to contradict him. He braked, then spun the car into a side road, hitting the kerb and coming to a stop. 'Get out.'

Ryan didn't need telling twice. He jumped out of the car. Three followed, still limping. The sirens were getting closer.

'What now? You can't even run!'

'But I can hide.' Three dropped to the ground, pulling his body under another car, a little further up the street. Ryan followed his lead.

Two seconds later, the police car turned into the road, screeching to a halt behind the stolen vehicle. From where they lay, Ryan could see the police officer's boots as they got out of their car.

'Vehicle abandoned in Garriden Road,' said a man, into his radio. 'It appears the boys have done a runner. But they can't have gone far. I'll have a look around.'

Ryan was sure his heartbeat would give them away. It sounded so loud as he lay there that it surprised him the officer hadn't heard it already.

The man seemed to take an age, checking out the gardens, asking the neighbours if they'd seen anything.

Finally, he returned to the vehicle, his shiny boots passing only a couple of feet from where the boys lay.

He spoke again into his radio. 'No sign of them. They've left the key in the vehicle. It's probably covered in prints. I'll lock it up and head back to the station.'

Ryan couldn't make out what the person at the other end said, but a few moments later, the officer climbed back into the police car and drove off.

'That was close,' muttered Three. 'Let's move before he comes back.'

They edged out from under the vehicle, and Ryan helped Three along as they made their way down the street.

'Do you know how we find the train station?' asked Ryan.

'I guess we keep heading into town and look for signs,' suggested Three.

But, they didn't get that far.

'Hello boys.' Firm hands grabbed them by the shoulders. 'Going somewhere?'

It turned out, the police officer wasn't as stupid as they thought. Instead of going back to the station, he'd parked in the next side road and waited to see if the culprits came out of hiding.

Ryan tried to twist away, but the officer pushed him against a wall and handcuffs clicked around his wrists. Three attempted to run while the officer was distracted, but with his wounded foot, he didn't get far.

A minute later, both boys were in the back of the police car.

The officer looked at them through the rear-view mirror. 'Haven't you boys been busy? I'm guessing you're the lads who were reported missing. Decide to do a bit of joyriding, did we?'

They both stayed silent.

There was nothing to say.

'How about we get you back to the station so I can get the paperwork done? Then you can go back where you belong.'

Ryan looked at Three.

Their escape attempt was over.

And they both knew what that meant.

They'd be taken to Blackfell.

And the governor would make them pay.

18. ALIVE

Shetford was only a small town and the police station was cramped.

Ryan and Three sat on plastic chairs, their hands cuffed behind them. It was impossible to get comfortable.

'I don't want you doing another runner now, do I?' said the police officer. He'd taken their fingerprints and filled out a crime report. Once that was done, he shouted over to a colleague. 'Can you remember who we contact about the missing boys from that young offenders' place?'

'I have the information here somewhere,' said his friend, shuffling the papers in a tray. It took him ages to find it. 'Here it is.'

The first officer looked up at Ryan and Three. 'Time to let them know where you are.'

'Please,' said Ryan, leaning forward, 'don't send us back there. You don't know what they do…'

Three jabbed Ryan in the ribs with his elbow. 'Be quiet,' he hissed.

'What do you mean?' asked the officer. He walked over to them.

Three shook his head. 'He just hates it there. That's all.'

'Is that true?'

Ryan nodded. 'I guess.'

The officer looked concerned. 'So, there's nothing you want to report?'

Three gave Ryan a warning look and gave a slight shake of his head.

Ryan took the hint. 'No.'

'In that case, I better phone them.'

The officer returned to his desk and picked up the phone. While he was busy chatting to the person on the other end, Ryan turned on Three.

'Why won't you let me tell him what they do to us? Some of that stuff *has* to be illegal. It might mean we don't get sent back there. It might get the place closed down.'

'It might,' allowed Three. 'But what if they still send us back there *after* we report them? Any idea what the governor will do then?'

'We're screwed anyway,' pointed out Ryan. 'It can't get any worse.'

'Trust me,' replied Three, a grim look on his face. 'It can *always* get worse.'

That wasn't a pleasant thought.

The police officer hung up the phone. 'They were glad to hear we'd got you. They're going to send someone to pick you up.'

'Fantastic.' Ryan couldn't hide the bitterness in his voice.

They'd gotten so far. He still believed that if Three hadn't been stupid enough to steal a car, they might have made it.

But there was no point dwelling on it.

They'd screwed up.

And now, they'd pay.

***

They didn't have to wait long.

A fierce-looking woman walked in to the station. She was wearing smart clothes and flashed an ID card at the officer. 'The governor sent me to collect the boys.'

The officer couldn't hide his surprise. 'Just you?'

She glared back at him as if to say 'What's your point?'

He didn't comment further, just shrugged and led her over to where the boys were sitting. 'Once I uncuff them, they might try to run,' he warned her.

'Don't worry. I brought my own.' She pulled two pairs of handcuffs from her handbag. 'Turn around, boys.'

Ryan and Three sighed and faced the wall, while the officer and the woman switched the cuffs. But something was nagging Ryan. It was the woman's voice. He'd heard it before.

Where do I know her from?

The woman signed some forms, then pushed the boys out of the station, gripping them by the shoulder. As soon as they were outside, she turned sharply to the left. Rather than taking them to a prison van, she walked over to a motorhome. 'Get in.'

Ryan climbed into the back, finding himself in a cramped seating area. There was a table and a tiny kitchenette. The place was in a state with screwed up paper and dirty cups littered around. Worse still, cigarette smoke hung in the air like a thick fog.

The boys slumped onto the brown seats while the woman started the engine.

She stepped on the accelerator so hard, Ryan fell sideways on to the floor. There was something weird about this entire setup. It didn't feel right.

'Who are you? Do you really work at Blackfell?' he asked, as they turned left, then right, making their way out of the town.

The woman glanced back at him. 'Who do you think rescued you?'

Ryan looked at Three and smiled. There was still hope. 'You sent the drone?'

'It was meant to bring you to me. What happened?'

'It crashed,' said Ryan.

'I wasn't expecting your friend to hitch a lift. It didn't have enough power to carry two of you.'

'My bad,' muttered Three. 'Maybe I should just have stayed in the Pen?'

'Maybe you should,' snapped the woman. 'As it is, you caused me no end of trouble. It's been near impossible keeping track of you through the woods. And now I have to cover my tracks.'

She sounded annoyed.

'How did you know where we were?' asked Three.

'I've been watching Blackfell for the last few days. Trying to find a way to get you out. I couldn't risk it until Ryan was outside on his own. In the end, I had to try it while the two of you were together.'

'I meant at the police station?'

'Oh, that. Police radio. Easy to intercept.'

That voice; where had Ryan heard it before?

He tried to hazard a guess. 'Did someone from Devonmoor Academy send you to rescue me?'

'You're kidding, right?' The woman shook her head. 'Those people don't care about you, Ryan. They'd have left you to rot at Blackfell. They're not your friends.'

Ryan wasn't sure that was true, but he didn't want to argue, not while he was handcuffed in the back of a vehicle with her at the wheel.

But the way she spoke about Devonmoor triggered something in Ryan's brain. It all clicked into place.

'The Outlier sent you.'

The woman snorted. 'I thought you were clever.'

Ryan's head spun. He could see the woman looking at him in the mirror, a strange smile on her face.

'Still not worked it out?' she asked.

'I give up.'

'I wasn't sent by the Outlier, Ryan. I *am* the Outlier.'

19. OPTIONS

Ryan didn't know what to say.

It couldn't be true.

Back at Devonmoor Academy, the Outlier was a legend. A former student who now hated the school, everyone spoke about them with hushed tones. Like Ryan, he was a hacker who never followed the rules. Last term, he had almost brought the Devonmoor family to its knees by draining their bank accounts, until Ryan had stopped him.

Him.

It was definitely *him*.

His real name was Sam Novak, Ryan knew that much. And when he had been at Devonmoor, he had been a boy. Ryan had even seen a picture.

Then, the Outlier had contacted Ryan, through a recording on the computer. And that's where Ryan had heard the voice before.

As his brain struggled to make sense of it, Ryan's mouth stumbled over his next words. 'But... but...'

You can't be.

'Aren't you going to say it, Ryan?'

Ryan was out of his depth. 'Say what?'

'That I can't be the Outlier, because I'm a woman.'

'Sam Novak was a boy.'

The woman laughed. 'Boy. Girl. Just because you're a hacker doesn't mean you have to think in binary.'

'I don't get it,' admitted Ryan. 'Are you the Outlier or not?' The motorhome turned a sharp corner and Ryan rolled around on the floor, narrowly avoiding a ketchup-smeared plate.

'I am. I already told you that. If you must know, I'm trans. Sometimes, I like to dress as a woman. Other times I identify as a man.'

'Oh.'

Through the windows, he could see a canopy of trees overhead. They were driving through the woods, away from Shetford.

'Where are you taking us?' asked Three.

'I haven't worked that out.'

'Do you think you can stop and get us out of these handcuffs,' pleaded Three.

'There's a layby up ahead. I'll pull over.'

***

A few minutes later, they were parked at the roadside and the boys were free of the cuffs. The Outlier slid aside a wooden panel, revealing a computer amid a stack of other technology which looked out of place in the cramped quarters.

'I need to check if we're being followed, and whether they know how you got away.' Her fingers moved like lightning over the keys and Ryan watched, fascinated, over her shoulder.

'Are you hacking the police database?'

'Just checking for updates. Nothing yet, which is perfect. They still haven't noticed anything amiss.'

She carried on tapping away.

'What are you doing now?' asked Three.

'Wiping the CCTV in the police station before they back it up. As soon as they realise I didn't come from Blackfell, they're going to want to find out who I am. I'd rather they didn't have any footage.'

'Clever.'

The Outlier gave Three a disdainful look. 'What *wasn't* clever was stealing a car. Do you have an IQ of ten? Did you *want* to make it as easy as possible for them to find you?'

Ryan looked over at Three. 'Told you.'

'We had to get away.'

'Fortunately, that made it easier for me to find you as well. I couldn't spot you, even with my drones.'

'You sent those? We thought the governor did.'

'It doesn't matter now.' The Outlier stood up. 'The police are clueless. I'm going to change into something more comfortable and then we can get going again.'

'Where to?' asked Ryan.

'Somewhere far away. Then we can plan our next move. There are drinks in the fridge if you're thirsty.' The Outlier disappeared into a door at the back of the van which led to a tiny bedroom. Ryan popped open the fridge door and held up a can of Coke. 'Want one?'

'Sure.' Three caught it as Ryan threw it to him. 'So, what happens now? We might have escaped but we're still outlaws.'

'I need to prove I'm innocent,' said Ryan. 'It's the only

way I'll get my life back.'

'How you planning to do that?'

'I'm not sure.' Ryan glanced over at the computer. 'I have to prove that Conrad Wolff framed me.'

'No, you don't.' The door opened, and the Outlier strode through, dressed in tight leather.

'Woah,' said Three.

'Something to say?' she asked, an edge to her voice.

Three paled. 'I just meant, err, you look good.'

'Why, thank you. If I'm ever looking for a thirteen-year-old boyfriend, I'll let you know.'

Three went bright red.

Ryan quickly changed the subject. 'Did you say I *don't* need to prove I'm innocent?' he asked.

'There's no point.' She sat down opposite the two boys. 'People like you and me, Ryan. We'll always be misunderstood. If you're not guilty of one thing, they just find something else to blame you for. It's best if you embrace it.'

'But then I'll go back to Blackfell.'

'Not if you stay with me. Remain invisible. Go off grid.'

'And live here?' Ryan looked around at the cramped quarters. He couldn't imagine spending the rest of his teenage years in a grimy motorhome.

The Outlier laughed. 'Sometimes. I don't live in it all the time. But I move around a lot.'

'What about Devonmoor Academy? And my family?'

'You don't need school, not with skills like yours. At the academy, they just want to make you into a little obedient cadet. Wear these clothes. Follow these rules.

Salute the teachers. Serve your country. You can be free of that. You can be rich. Change your identity. Live where you like. Do what you like.'

She had a point, but Ryan wasn't convinced.

'My friends are there.'

'I'm not sure you're that popular right now,' pointed out the Outlier. 'They think you're responsible for the death of those other cadets.'

'Not all of them. Else you wouldn't be here.'

'Anyone care to fill me in?' asked Three.

Ryan took pity on him. 'I got one of my best friends, Lee, to message the Outlier, to tell him, err, her, that I was being taken to Blackfell and needed help.'

'You'll need more than a few friends to get you out of the trouble you're in,' said the Outlier. 'It would be much easier to stay off grid.'

'But then I'll never be able to see my parents.'

'True. But do they care about you?'

'Of course.' Ryan said it a little too forcefully.

The Outlier shifted in her seat. 'If you're sure.'

'I am sure.' Another awkward pause.

Then Three spoke. 'I hate to interrupt, but what happens to *me*?'

The Outlier leaned back and lit a cigarette. 'That's a good question, Dick.'

Three pulled a face. 'Please don't call me that.'

'It's your name. It's on all the crime reports.'

'I prefer being called Three.'

'I can see why,' quipped Ryan, grinning. 'I wondered why you wouldn't tell me your real name.'

Three looked away, embarrassed.

The Outlier shrugged. 'I suppose I can get you back to your family.'

'No thanks! My stepdad will just send me straight back to Blackfell. I can't ever go there again.'

'Can you hack?' asked the Outlier.

'That's one reason they locked me up.'

'I might find a use for you.' She blew a cloud of smoke in his face.

Three gulped; he didn't like the sound of that.

Ryan felt a little for the boy. But right now, he had enough problems of his own. 'I'm grateful for the offer and everything,' he said to the Outlier, 'but I want to take down Wolff. He deserves to pay.'

'Ah, revenge.' The Outlier nodded. '*That* I can understand.'

'So, you'll help me?'

'I'll do what I can.'

20. PLAN

They drove for hours.

During the journey, Ryan explained to Three about Devonmoor Academy and how he knew the Outlier.

'That's some history,' said Three, glancing over at the woman driving. 'But what do we call you? I mean, do you prefer *Sir* or *Miss* or what?'

The Outlier laughed. 'You're not at school now. Or in prison. You can call me Sam.'

'Sure. Ok.'

Ryan couldn't hold his curiosity any longer. 'When did you know you were trans? When you left Devonmoor?'

'Long before that. The other kids used to bully me about being effeminate. Well, not just the kids.'

Things started to click into place. 'Colonel Keller. I bet that's why he hated you so much. Because you were different.'

'He belongs in another time. He can't cope when people don't fit into his neat little boxes. In his world, men should be men, whatever that means.'

'But you prefer being a woman?' Three blurted it out.

Sam didn't look offended. 'Sometimes.'

That shut Three up. He'd never known anyone like her before.

They drove down a motorway, before turning on to smaller roads that led through the countryside. After a while, they pulled into a small muddy car park in the middle of some woods.

'I think we'll be safe here.' Sam joined the boys in the back of the van, settling down on to the comfortable seating. Her leather trousers made a strange noise as she crossed her legs. 'Now, we need a plan. And if it involves taking down someone as clever as Conrad Wolff, it better be good.'

'I've been thinking about that for days before you rescued me,' said Ryan.

Sam gave a thin smile. 'Plotting your revenge. We're more similar than you realise.'

Ryan shifted in his seat; he wasn't sure he liked the comparison. 'Just before he tried to kill me, Wolff told me he had a son around my age.'

'And?'

'It has to be his weak spot, right? I mean, he's surrounded by Level Five security at his offices, and has bodyguards wherever he goes. But his son can't be kept safe all the time.'

'So, we kidnap him?' cut in Three. 'Hold him hostage until Wolff admits he framed you?'

'Possibly,' admitted Ryan. 'I haven't figured out all the details.'

Sam shook her head. 'It won't work. Even if Wolff admitted something to get his son back, it wouldn't be worth anything. He could just claim he was lying to save his son's life. What father wouldn't do that?'

'I guess it's a stupid idea.'

'Maybe.' Sam looked away, deep in thought. 'But you might be on to something about Wolff's son being the weak link.'

'What do you mean?'

'Let me check something.'

Ryan and Three sat in silence while Sam took her place in front of the computer.

After a while, Ryan felt he should say something. 'Find anything useful?'

'You're right about Wolff's son. Twelve years old. He's called Jasper. Spoiled little brat by the look of him. Goes to some posh school in London.'

'A boarding school?'

Sam tapped away some more before answering. 'No. He lives at home with his dad. Travels in every day.'

That surprised Ryan.

Three cut in. 'How does that help us?'

'Because information is always useful,' snapped Sam. 'And as the lowest IQ in the room, it would also help if you stayed quiet while we try to think.'

'Sorry for breathing,' muttered Three.

Ryan gave him an apologetic look. 'What if we didn't kidnap him? What if I became friends with him? Maybe I could get invited to his house. If I could get to Wolff's home office, I might be able to find something I could use.'

'Too vague,' said Sam. 'The evidence you're after won't be sitting on his computer. And even if it is, Wolff will have protection that even we can't crack. Not that fast, anyway.'

A moment of silence.

Ryan's brain was buzzing with ideas, trying to work out the best way to prove his innocence. And suddenly it came to him. It was possibly the craziest idea he'd ever had.

He looked up at the others. 'I think I know what we need to do...'

***

'It might just work.' The Outlier lit another cigarette as she mulled over Ryan's plan. 'It's a hell of a risk, but it's not impossible.'

'Where do we start?' asked Ryan.

'We have to get you a place at the same school as Wolff's son. But first, we need a new name and a bit of personal history. I'll pull up some randomly generated names and we'll pick one out.'

The Outlier tapped away, and a list appeared on the screen.

'Ben,' suggested Ryan. 'I reckon that would suit me.'

But Sam shook her head. 'Too common. You need something that rich people would use.'

'Hugo,' said Three, grinning.

'No way,' shot back Ryan.

'Albert?'

'Are you trying to wind me up?'

Sam looked up. 'What about Jacob? It's your surname, so you're used to it already.'

'Makes sense,' agreed Ryan. 'It's better than most of the others. But what about my surname?'

'We'll go for something double-barrelled. Let's see

what the random generator comes up with.'

A list of twenty surnames appeared on the screen.

'Any you like?' asked Sam.

'Not really,' admitted Ryan. 'But I guess that would work.' He pointed to the screen at Jacob Farley-Harrington.

'Do you *want* to get bullied?' asked Three.

'It's not like that,' explained Sam. 'It's not that sort of school. Everyone will have posh names. He'll fit right in. Jacob Farley-Harrington it is.'

'Don't you think they'll think it's weird, joining in June?' pointed out Three. 'The year is almost over. Not the time you'd expect someone to move school.'

Sam nodded. 'Those details matter. Let's build it into the backstory. Jacob's mum is desperate for him to get started as soon as possible. She's obsessed with his education and doesn't want him missing out on any work they set over the summer.'

'My mum?' asked Ryan.

'Yes, me.' The Outlier winked at Ryan. 'I'll be registering you, signing your forms, paying your tuition.'

'Won't that cost a lot?'

'It's just money. I can always get money.'

It turned out, that was a good thing because even the uniform at St Oswald's cost a fortune.

'Am I gonna have to wear *that*,' said Ryan, wincing at the yellow and black striped blazer and tie on the screen. 'It's revolting.'

Sam shrugged. 'The more expensive the school, the worse the uniform.'

'You're not kidding.'

'We'll have to change your date of birth, to make sure you end up in the same school year as Jasper. Otherwise, he'll be in the year below you.'

'Good job I'm small for my age.'

Sam filled in the details, speeding through the application. Before submitting it, she turned to Ryan. 'It's a huge risk, what you're about to do. It might land you back in Blackfell. By now, I'd bet they've put stuff in place to prevent others being rescued the same way. You can still back out and just live off grid with me. You sure you want to do this?'

Ryan took a deep breath, but he knew he couldn't spend his whole life on the run. 'One hundred percent.'

Sam turned back to the online application and clicked 'Submit.'

21. INTELLIGENCE

The daylight was fading by the time they finished.

'I don't want to be rude, but do you have any food?' asked Three. 'I'm starving.'

'Yeah, I could use something to eat,' admitted Ryan. 'We haven't had anything since breakfast.'

Sam stood up and walked over to the kitchenette. 'I'm afraid I'm not much of a cook. Never learned how. I eat the same thing every day.'

'What's that?' asked Three.

She opened the cupboard. It was stacked with identical tins. 'Hot dogs.'

'Got any rolls to go with those?' asked Three.

'There should be some around here somewhere.' Sam hunted around in the pile of stuff on the kitchen worktop. 'Here we are. I think they'll be ok.' She opened a tin and placed some of the slimy sausages on a plate in the microwave. 'That's the thing about growing up in a place like Devonmoor. You don't learn basic life skills, like cooking.'

'How long is it since you left?' asked Ryan, curious. He was finding it hard to estimate Sam's age.

'Four years.'

The answer surprised Ryan. Sam looked way older than that.

'Don't you get bored, living on your own?' asked Three, glancing around.

Ryan knew what Three was thinking. It didn't look much, living in the filthy van. But Sam looked up, confused. 'Bored? No way. I have all the time I need to work on my programs without distractions. Whenever I want a change of scenery, I move on.'

Sam reminded Ryan of Mr Davids, the computer teacher at Devonmoor Academy. Hackers liked to be alone with their machines.

She tore open the bread rolls with her hands and stuffed the hot dogs inside before handing it to the boys without a plate.

'Err, thanks,' said Three.

Ryan looked down at his own food. The bread was dry and he could see flecks of mould, but he was hungry enough to ignore it. He took a bite.

'Do you spend all day hacking?' he asked.

Sam collapsed in her seat as though preparing the hot dogs had been a major effort. 'No, I'm working on something much more exciting than that.'

Ryan took the bait. 'What is it?'

'Artificial intelligence, Ryan. The ultimate prize.'

'Huh?' Three looked confused.

'She's trying to create a computer that's as intelligent as us,' explained Ryan. 'That can think and act like a human.'

'Not quite,' corrected Sam, her eyes twinkling. 'It will be *more* intelligent than us.'

'You sure that's a good idea?' asked Three. 'Have you never watched the *Terminator* movies?'

Sam held up her hand. 'Hollywood trash. True super-intelligence is a thing of beauty. Think of all those problems that people can't solve: climate change, poverty, disease. Our best people spend years hoping for the tiniest breakthrough, but the size of their brains limits them. *Deep Reach* will change all of that, when she's ready.'

'She?' Three raised his eyebrows.

'Yes, she. Deep Reach won't be an abstract intelligence. She will have personality too. Emotion. A desire to create. She will be humanity's biggest achievement.'

'Aren't you a bit late?' pointed out Three. 'Hasn't it already been done?'

Sam snorted. 'They've made some breakthroughs in the last few years. Mostly clever language and image processing. Nothing on this level.'

Even Ryan was finding it hard to hide his disbelief. 'How long will it take you to finish the program?'

Sam stared out of the window into the darkness. 'Hard to say. It needs a specialist piece of hardware. Something unique. Until I have it, *Deep Reach* is just a lot of code.'

Three glanced over. Ryan knew what he was thinking: this woman is crazy. But Ryan had seen this kind of obsession before. It was normal for a genius; they lived in a different world. Sam could be deluding herself about her chances of success, but she'd been at Devonmoor Academy and that had to count for something. Only the best and the brightest kids went there.

'You need the Fractal Processor,' muttered Ryan.

The Outlier leaned forward. 'You know about that? Can you get it for me? When you get back to Devonmoor.'

Ryan shook his head. 'I don't know where it is. Mr Davids keeps it hidden. Even the other teachers don't know the location.'

'But you could find out?'

Ryan didn't want to commit to stealing the chip from the academy for the Outlier, but he was worried that if he refused outright, she would no longer help to clear his name.

'I could try.' He felt guilty just saying it.

'Good.'

Having finished his food, Three yawned. 'I don't know about you two, but I'm beat.'

'Me too,' admitted Ryan. 'We barely slept last night. I think we've been running on pure adrenaline.'

Sam kicked some stuff to the side. 'This seat pulls out into a bed, but you'll have to share.'

'Hey, as long as it has a mattress, I'll be fine.'

'Oh yeah, I forgot about that.' Three grinned at Ryan. 'You'll sleep like a baby tonight.'

The boys used cushions from the sofa as pillows and Sam threw them an old blanket. 'Sleep well, boys.' She retreated to the back of the van and closed the door.

Ryan used the tiny bathroom, then lay down next to Three. The mattress was thin, but after his time at Blackfell, he wasn't about to complain.

'You know your friend is a few cards short of a full deck, right?' murmured Three. 'Total looney-toon.'

'Maybe. But she rescued us, didn't she?'

'She's probably drugged us as well. Don't be surprised if you wake up chained in a basement.'

Ryan punched him on the arm. 'Relax, will you? She's ok. But if you want to fantasise about being chained in her basement, you go ahead.'

Three huffed. 'Don't say I didn't warn you.'

Ryan wondered whether Three had a point. How well did they know Sam, really? No, she might be an oddball, but he felt safer in her motorhome than he had felt for weeks. Besides, he knew what she wanted.

She'd help him prove his innocence. And then she'd want him to return the favour by getting hold of the Fractal Processor.

One problem at a time, Ryan.

He couldn't do anything about that right now; it was late, and he was too tired to think.

He drifted off into an uneasy sleep.

22. RAIN

Ryan rubbed his eyes and sat up.

It was still dark and he could hear rain drumming against the roof of the van. Three was already awake, sitting at the computer, tapping away.

'What are you doing?' hissed Ryan.

Three swivelled around, his finger pressed against his lips. 'Shh. You'll wake up the crazy lady.'

'She won't want you on her computer,' whispered Ryan.

'I know that.' Three turned back to the screen. 'But I thought we could find a few things out. Verify her story, just in case. And I'm curious to see what this *Deep Reach* thing looks like.'

Ryan shuffled over in the narrow quarters. He was so frustrated, he could barely keep his voice down. 'If she finds out you're messing with her hardware, she'll kill you.'

And she won't help me to clear my name.

That's what he wanted to say, but he guessed Three wouldn't care about that.

'I'll take that risk.' Three was rebooting the machine, attempting to bypass the security login. 'In case you forgot, we're hackers. It's what we do.'

Ryan couldn't believe Three was about to ruin

everything and betray the person who'd helped them escape. He stood behind the blond kid and gripped his shoulders tightly. 'Turn off the computer off. Now.'

'No way. Stop being a wuss.'

That did it. Ryan reached over and hit the switch, killing the power.

'You shouldn't have done that.' Three jumped up and pushed Ryan back. He fell against the kitchenette, and as he tried to steady himself, he knocked some plates on to the floor. One of them smashed.

The door to the bedroom flew open and light flooded the small space.

'WHAT is going on here.' Sam stood over them, her face like thunder.

Ryan looked at Three. 'You want to tell her?'

He shrugged. 'I was trying to hack into your computer. To find out what's on there and see if you're telling the truth.'

The Outlier moved faster than Ryan could believe. She leapt over the bed and grabbed Three by the throat, slamming him against the side of the van. 'You NEVER touch my computer without permission. Do you hear me?'

Three could barely speak. 'I hear you,' he gasped.

'I tried to stop him,' added Ryan, keen to distance himself from Three's stupidity.

Sam dragged Three towards the door. 'Give me one good reason why I shouldn't throw you out of my van right now.'

'I'm only wearing boxers,' gasped Three, his eyes wide.

'I said a *good* reason.' Sam flung open the van door and threw the lad out into the storm. 'You can walk home from here.' With that, she slammed the door.

Ryan glanced out the window, horrified. He could see Three sprawled on the grass, rain hammering against his bare skin. 'You can't leave him out there.'

'Can't I?' The Outlier raised her eyebrows, as if daring him to contradict her. She made her way through to the bedroom and started getting dressed.

'He's virtually naked,' pointed out Ryan. 'He could get hypothermia and die.'

'And the world will be rid of one more stupid person.'

Ryan's brain was working overtime. He knew Three had overstepped the mark by trying to hack into the Outlier's computer, but he didn't think the kid deserved this. 'We need him,' he reminded her, 'for the plan. And if anyone finds him, we don't know what he'll tell them.'

Sam frowned. 'I suppose you're right.' She made her way back over to the van door and slid it open. 'You're a lucky boy,' she called out to Three. 'Ryan has persuaded me to let you back in.'

Three shuffled towards the van. As he stepped inside, rain dripped from his hair.

Sam threw him the manky towel from next to the sink. 'If you ever touch my machine again without permission, I'll chop off your hands.'

Given what had just happened, Ryan wasn't even sure that was an exaggeration.

Either way, it seemed that Three had got the message. 'Noted,' said the boy, as he dried off.

'Well, as we're all awake, I suppose we better get

moving,' said the Outlier, pushing her way past to the driver's seat. 'We need to get to London to buy your uniform and get some supplies.'

'When do I start at St Oswalds?' asked Ryan. He knew that the longer he had to wait, the more nervous he would be.

'Thursday.' The Outlier started the engine and turned on the headlights.

Two days.

That didn't sound too bad.

With a sudden lurch, the motorhome shot forwards, throwing both boys back on to the bed.

Three glanced over at Ryan. 'Thanks for making her let me back in,' he muttered.

Ryan punched Three on the arm. 'Yeah, well next time I tell you something, how about you listen?'

Three pulled a face. 'I'll try, but I'm not making any promises.'

***

It took a long time to get to London.

When they arrived at their destination, Sam told the boys to stay in the van while she went shopping for Ryan's uniform.

'Why can't I come with you?' Ryan asked. He was bored of being stuck inside, especially after hours travelling down the motorway.

'Too risky,' said the Outlier. 'I don't know if the police are on the lookout for a woman with two boys your age.'

'So why don't you dress as a man?' suggested

Three. 'That's what you do, isn't it?'

'I'm not feeling it today,' said Sam. 'I have to listen to my body. I can't just decide.'

From the look on Three's face, Ryan could tell the boy was about to say something stupid. He gave him a warning glance. 'Can't I come with you, though?' asked Ryan. 'Three can stay here.'

Sam snorted. 'I'm not leaving that punk alone with my equipment. I'm trusting you to keep an eye on him. Keep the curtains drawn. I won't be long.'

With that, she was gone.

Three sneaked a peek out of the window. 'You realise we could take another shot at hacking into her computer?'

'We're not doing that.' Ryan's voice was hard. He wondered if he was going to have to physically restrain his friend.

But when Three turned around to face him, he was smiling. 'Relax. I'm just kidding.'

Ryan threw a screwed up piece of paper at him. 'You had me worried there for a second,' he admitted.

'Bit extreme, though, isn't she?' mused Three.

'I'm just glad she's on our side.'

'Yeah. Until she chops off our hands.'

***

Sam was only gone for an hour. When she returned, she had bags full of school uniform. 'Here,' she said to Ryan. 'You need to try these on.'

A few minutes later, Ryan emerged from the

bedroom, dressed in the St Oswalds uniform. He felt like a total idiot. It looked even worse in real life than it had done on the screen.

There was no way anyone should have to wear a yellow shirt and a black-and-yellow striped blazer. It was a crime against decency. Even the black trousers had a pinstripe.

Three burst out laughing. 'That's worse than anything they did to us at Blackfell.'

'Tell me about it,' replied Ryan, miserably.

'At least it fits,' pointed out Sam, trying not to smile.

'It itches like crazy.' Ryan pulled on the tie.

'You look like such a nerd,' teased Three.

'Hey, you still need to try on *yours*,' said Sam, throwing a bag over to him.

'Fine by me.' Three didn't even bother to disappear into the bedroom. He changed where he was, pulling on a plain white shirt, grey trousers and a navy-blue jumper.

'His is nowhere near as bad,' complained Ryan.

'That's because I'm not going to St Oswalds, am I?' pointed out Three. 'And I'm only wearing this to help you out, so quit your moaning.'

It was true. For the plan to work, Three had to look like he attended a different school.

'Can I take this off now?' asked Ryan.

Sam nodded. 'Until Thursday.'

Ryan stepped back into the cramped bedroom and stripped off the clothes as fast as he could.

All he could think about was that in less than two days time, he would be riding the bus to St Oswalds, and his mission would truly begin.

23. BUS

It felt weird, being in the city.

Devonmoor Academy was such a secluded place and Blackfell had been in the middle of nowhere. Even Ryan's home was in the suburbs of a large town. But the bus-stop was surrounded by tall buildings and busy roads. There was so much activity, it put Ryan on edge.

He felt stupid, wearing the yellow and black uniform in public. Thankfully, he wasn't the only one. A few other kids were heading to St Oswalds. They gave him wary looks, wondering why they'd never seen him before.

'You new?' asked an older girl. She was taller than him, with neat brown hair tied into a ponytail.

'First day,' admitted Ryan. 'Not sure I'm looking forward to it. What's it like?'

She shrugged. 'S'ok, I guess. They give you tons of homework and some teachers are strict. But no worse than anywhere else. Where was your last place?'

Ryan hesitated for a second, then remembered his backstory. 'Marlowe School. It's a private school in Surrey. But my mum got a new job in London.'

'What year are you in?' asked a geeky-looking boy with glasses.

'Nine.'

'Me too. My name's Cedric.'

Ryan almost made the mistake of saying his real name. This was going to be trickier than he thought. 'Jacob.'

Cedric held out his hand, which seemed stupidly formal for a meeting between schoolkids, but Ryan shook it anyway.

'Kate,' said the taller girl, also offering him her hand.

Ryan already felt like an imposter. Pretending to be a student here would be a hard sell. At least the other students were talking to him. Maybe Jasper would be just as keen to make friends.

'Here's our bus,' pointed out Cedric, as a double-decker crawled along the road towards them and pulled over at the stop.

Ryan climbed aboard to find most of the seats were taken. It seemed like everyone had their usual place.

'You can sit next to me,' offered Cedric, as he slumped down two rows from the front.

Ryan wasn't sure that was a good idea. Even though he'd only just met Cedric, he had a feeling that hanging around with him would be social suicide. But it wasn't like he had much choice; there was nowhere else to sit.

'Thanks,' he said, perching on the edge of the seat and twisting his body away from Cedric as much as he could without causing offence.

Back in the motorhome, they'd worked out that Jasper Wolff travelled to school on this same bus. He'd be getting on in a couple of minutes. That's why they'd chosen this route for Ryan's journey to school. With any luck, that might give them more opportunities to connect.

Sure enough, Jasper climbed aboard a few stops later.

The kid strutted on as though he owned the place, his hair slicked back, his sharp eyes scanning the seats. For a moment he stared at Ryan. Then, he made his way over.

To Ryan's surprise, Cedric had already stood up and was rummaging around in his satchel.

'Excuse me, Jacob,' he said. 'I need to let Jasper sit down.'

'You do,' grinned Jasper. 'I assume you got it done?'

Cedric nodded. He handed over two exercise books. In return, Jasper handed over some cash.

'Good boy.' Jasper ruffled Cedric's hair, then pushed past Ryan and flopped down next to him in the window seat. Cedric was left standing in the aisle.

'You pay him to do your homework?' asked Ryan.

Jasper narrowed his eyes. 'What's it to you, new boy? Not a grass, are you?'

Ryan snorted. 'No chance. It's none of my business. I was just curious.'

'Good.' Jasper looked out the window for a moment, and Ryan wondered if the conversation was over. But then he turned back. 'I'm Jasper.'

'Jacob.'

'Why are you starting at St Oswalds?'

Ryan used the same backstory as before, but added a few details. 'Mum moved here for her work, and she wanted me to have a new start. I kept getting into trouble at my last place.'

It was the right thing to say.

Jasper grinned. 'You know what, Jacob. I already like you.'

'Thanks.' Ryan tried to appear casual but he couldn't believe his luck. He'd been worried that it would be difficult to befriend Jasper. He'd never dreamed that they'd hit it off before they reached the school gates.

Now, he just had to make sure he didn't blow it, so he could enact the second part of the plan.

***

The bus pulled up outside the school.

It was one of those buildings that looked old, like it was built two hundred years ago. A wall of trees and bushes protected it from the city streets.

'Mum said I have to report to the office,' said Ryan.

'Want me to come with you?' asked Jasper.

'Sure.' The way Ryan figured it, the more time he spent with Jasper the better. He needed to get close to him, so he'd eventually get invited to Jasper's house.

'This way.' Jasper led Ryan around the front of the building, away from the other students.

They climbed some grand steps. A large wooden door stood between two pillars, and Jasper pushed it open. Inside was a plush reception area with comfortable seating and glossy prospectuses. A large trophy cabinet dominated the far end, showing off the school's many achievements. To their right was a surprisingly modern reception desk.

A grey-haired lady looked up at them. 'Wrong entrance, boys.'

Jasper gave her a patronising smile. 'Actually, it's not. Jacob is meant to report to the office as it's his first day. I thought I'd show him where it was.'

For whatever reason, the lady didn't seem to like Jasper much. Her eyes narrowed. 'How kind of you.' She turned to Ryan. 'You must be Jacob Farley-Harrington.'

'Farley-Harrington?' laughed Jasper. 'That's a proper rich brat's name.'

Ryan blushed, wishing they'd chosen something plainer. 'I know.' Then he turned on Jasper, as if looking for ammunition of his own. 'What's your surname, then?'

Jasper smiled. 'Wolff.'

'Oh. That's actually decent.'

That seemed to make Jasper happy. 'Farley-Harrington's decent too, if you spend your weekend hunting foxes.' He gave Ryan a playful shove.

The woman behind the desk handed over a timetable. 'It looks like your parents have submitted everything we need. This is your schedule. I imagine Jasper will be happy to show you around?'

Jasper gave her another sickly sweet smile. 'Of course, Mrs Butterworth.' He snatched the timetable out of Ryan's hands. 'We have loads of the same lessons.'

That wasn't a surprise to Ryan. The Outlier had hacked into the school's computer system the night before to make sure of that.

'I hope you have a lovely time here, Jacob,' said the receptionist. 'Try to stay out of trouble.'

That seemed like a strange thing to say to a kid on their first day, but Ryan nodded. 'I'll try.'

The woman looked like she was going to say something else, but she hesitated, and Jasper pulled Ryan away.

'Come on,' he said. 'You wouldn't want to be late for registration.'

24. CASH

It seemed like Jasper owned the school.

As they walked down the corridor, kids moved out of the way.

'Are they scared of you?' asked Ryan.

Jasper grinned. 'Yeah, unless they're stupid.'

'Why's that?'

'Because they know I'm in charge.'

'Aren't you worried the teachers will find out?'

'I don't threaten them, Jacob. I pay them for their services.' Jasper paused for a moment. 'What did you get in trouble for? At your last school?'

'Usual stuff. Skiving. Fighting. Swearing at a teacher.'

Jasper nodded as if he approved. 'You a tough guy?'

Ryan shrugged. 'I can hold my own.'

'They won't let you get away with any of that stuff here. Not if they know about it. You have to be clever.'

Ryan was about to ask how, but Jasper was distracted. An Asian boy was walking in their direction, his head down as if he was trying hard not to be noticed. It didn't work.

'Ah, Eesah!' Jasper greeted him like his best friend, putting an arm around the boy's shoulder. 'I've been meaning to speak with you.'

Eesah gulped. 'What do you want, Jasper?'

'You been studying hard for the maths test this afternoon?'

'Of course.'

'Good. Then do me a favour, will you? Write my name at the top of your paper.' Jasper reached into his pocket and pulled out a wad of notes.

Eesah looked at it longingly.

'There's nothing to worry about,' soothed Jasper, forcing the money into his hand. 'I'll write your name on my paper. So, it's all ok, isn't it?'

'But what if we get caught?'

'We won't. As long as you do what I say. If not, there will be two papers with your name on them and none with mine. And that won't end well for either of us. Especially for you.'

'I don't know, Jasper.' Eesah tried to pull away. 'Can't you get someone else to do it?'

'I could, but I've chosen you. Don't let me down, now. I'm expecting an A.'

Eesah backed away. 'I'll do my best.'

As soon as he was gone, Jasper turned back to Ryan. 'He's here on a scholarship. His mum can hardly afford the uniform. He only owns one blazer. He'll do anything for cash.'

Ryan looked down. He had to play this right. 'I'm not that rich myself. Not since my dad left.'

'How does your mum afford the fees?'

'She doesn't. My grandparents pay those. It's tough surviving on Mum's salary.'

Jasper's eyes lit up. 'Well, maybe you'd like to earn

a little cash of your own?'

'How?'

'I'll think of something.' Jasper's lip curled. He was already thinking through the possibilities, working out how he could fit Ryan into his little scheme.

But that suited Ryan just fine.

If Jasper knew Ryan needed his money, he'd be less likely to see him as a threat.

***

Lessons at St Oswalds were boring and predictable. The teachers expected the kids to sit quietly and do as they were told.

But being friends with Jasper had its advantages. He let Ryan sit next to him at the back of the class. They played hangman while the teacher droned on.

In maths, they couldn't do that because of the test, but when Ryan glanced over, he saw Jasper had written Eesah's name at the top of his paper, just before he handed it in.

'Don't the teachers recognise your handwriting?' Ryan asked him as soon as the lesson was over.

'If they do, they turn a blind eye. They want me to have good marks, to keep my dad on side.'

'What about Eesah's parents?'

'Eesah's father isn't about to pay for a new science block. He'll get grounded or something. Nothing too serious.'

As they reached the canteen, Jasper walked straight to the front of the queue and grabbed a tray off a younger kid.

'Take this kid's tray,' he said to Ryan, nodding towards the skinny lad next to him. Ryan did as he was told, snatching it from his hands.

'I think you boys missed the trays,' said Jasper. 'You better go to the back of the line.'

'Or what?'

'Or I'll pay someone to teach you a lesson.'

The lads lowered their heads and slouched off.

'Just one advantage of being with me,' said Jasper. 'You never have to queue for lunch.'

'Suits me,' said Ryan. He felt sorry for the boys, but couldn't let it show.

The food at St Oswalds was decent. After nearly starving to death at Blackfell, and then having to cope with the random offerings at the motorhome, Ryan's mouth watered as the canteen staff loaded his plate with roast chicken, potatoes and veg. There was even a Yorkshire pudding. He followed Jasper to a table.

'So, Jacob Farley-Harrington,' said Jasper, as he chewed on his chicken, 'I'm wondering what you'd do for five hundred quid.'

Ryan almost choked on his food. 'What?'

'I like you, Jacob. I think we're going to be friends. And I'd like to help you out. You need money, right? Well, I have loads. But I can't just give it to you. That's not how it works. You have to earn it.'

'How?'

'You say you're a bad boy? A rebel?'

Ryan didn't like where this was going. 'I guess.'

'We don't get many of those here.'

144

'So?'

'So, if I want the afternoon off and need someone to phone up the school with a fake bomb threat, would you do it?'

'Maybe.' Ryan was non-committal. If he got caught and expelled, he wouldn't be able to stay friends with Jasper.

'What if I want you to set fire to the school?'

Ryan squirmed. 'People could die.'

Jasper grinned. 'Say it was empty. At night.'

'I'd need a lot more than five hundred.'

'What if I need you to beat some kid up?'

Ryan stalled for time. 'Depends on the kid.'

'Here's what I think. You need to prove you're not all talk. I need to know if you're as much of a tough guy as you say you are.'

Ryan leaned back and looked him in the eye. 'That's fair. What exactly do you have in mind?'

25. REVENGE

'You see the lad with the ginger hair sitting next to the vending machine?'

Ryan glanced over. 'Yeah. What about him?'

'That's Troy, captain of the school football team.' Jasper pulled a face, as if just saying the boy's name disgusted him. 'I want you to break his legs.'

Ryan almost spat out his drink. 'What?'

Jasper stared him down. 'You heard me.'

'What did he do to you?'

'I asked him to speak to the coach, to get me on the team, and he refused. He told me I wasn't good enough. So, I told him that if I couldn't play, he wouldn't either.'

'That's nothing to do with me,' said Ryan evenly. 'I thought you were going to ask me to steal or vandalise something. I'm not breaking anyone's legs.'

Jasper stood up and picked up his tray, about to move to another table. 'I knew you were all talk.'

Ryan could see his opportunity to befriend Jasper slipping away. He had to rescue the situation, and fast. 'It's not that I'm not up for it. It's just I can't see any way I could do that. Not without getting caught.'

Jasper hesitated and sat back down. 'We've got hockey in PE this afternoon. All it would take is one bad tackle.'

'It's not that easy,' said Ryan. 'Breaking someone's legs isn't as straightforward as it sounds.'

'You only have to break one of them,' said Jasper, as if that was a major compromise. 'Just make sure he can't play in the match tomorrow.'

'If I take him out that badly, they'll know I did it deliberately.'

Jasper narrowed his eyes. 'You're just making excuses.'

'No. I'm speaking facts. But there might be something else we could do.'

'You,' said Jasper. 'I can't get involved in this. It will be too obvious.'

'If I find a way to injure him, what do I get out of it?' asked Ryan.

Jasper gave a sly smile. 'Five hundred quid. And my respect.'

'Five hundred?' Ryan mulled it over.

'Do we have a deal?' asked Jasper.

Ryan sighed. 'Sure.'

***

The changing room was crammed with boys. Ryan could barely find space to put his bag, but he forced himself between two geeky kids.

The St Oswalds sports kit wasn't that much better than the uniform. There was a rugby top with black and yellow hoops, and the socks were the same. It made the boys look like bumblebees.

Ryan could see Troy opposite, pulling on industrial

quality shin guards. This was a boy that didn't like to take chances. His legs would be better protected than a tank. Injuring him would be almost impossible.

Almost.

Think, Ryan, think.

Out of the corner of his eye, he could see Jasper glancing over at him as he pulled on his shirt. If Ryan didn't find a way to put Troy out of action, his mission to befriend Jasper would be in tatters. There had to be something he could do.

As the boys started heading outside, Ryan hung back, relacing his football boots. He needed more time to think. Jasper gave him a quizzical look as he passed, but he said nothing.

There was no way he could go through with Jasper's plan. Even if Ryan smashed his stick full force against Troy's legs, there wasn't much chance of breaking them, not with the amount of protection he was wearing.

What, then?

As Ryan looked around the empty changing room, he had an idea. He knew exactly what he needed to do. But he needed to be quick.

***

By the time Ryan joined the rest of the students out on the field, they were doing laps.

'You're late,' said the coach, frowning at him. 'Are you new? I don't remember seeing you before.'

'Yes, sir. Started today.'

'What's your name?'

'Jacob Farley-Harrington.'

'Well, Jacob, as it's your first day, I'll let you off. But in the future, you'll need to get changed faster. Do you understand?'

'Yes, sir.'

'Ok, do a lap. And be quick.'

Ryan jogged off, wondering if his plan would work.

When everyone had finished warming up, they were split into two teams. Ryan was put on the opposite team to Troy. That meant, in theory at least, Ryan could take the boy out in a messy challenge.

Ryan felt the weight of the hockey stick. It was some weapon. Troy might be wearing shin guards, but if he was cracked hard on the knee, it would do some serious damage.

But, no. It would still be pretty obvious. Everyone would know it was his clumsy challenge that had taken Troy out. And he had no desire to cripple him. It was too severe, whatever Jasper said.

But neither could Ryan afford to lose his chance at staying close to Jasper. He had to win him over and prove he was tough enough for them to be friends.

It would have been an enjoyable match, if it wasn't for the stress. Ryan had never been into hockey, but he didn't hate it either. The problem was that as the game progressed, Jasper kept giving him sharp looks, as if urging him to take action.

There was one moment where Ryan could have done it. Troy was hurtling down the pitch with the ball and Ryan faced him off in defence. With the speed Troy was going, a wild swing with the stick would certainly have caused some damage.

Instead, Ryan opted for a fair tackle, trying to block Troy as he made his way up the field. He got the ball, but that hardly mattered, given what was at stake.

'What are you waiting for?' hissed Jasper, jogging past.

'Just trust me, ok?' said Ryan.

'You might not get another opportunity like that,' murmured Jasper. 'I knew you'd bottle it.'

Ryan did his best to ignore Jasper for the rest of the match. And while he had a couple more opportunities to tackle Troy, he didn't make any attempt to injure him.

When the final whistle blew, Jasper fell in line next to Ryan. 'You're a waste of space, Farley-Harrington. I thought we had a deal.'

'We do. Just wait.'

That got a confused look, but Jasper couldn't say anything else, as too many other boys were nearby, so they walked back to the changing room in silence.

A wall of noise greeted them as they entered: the hiss of hot showers, the banging of football boots, the general banter and mayhem of post-match rivalry. Ryan kept a close eye on Troy as he changed into his school uniform.

There was a moment of chaos as one boy realised his phone was missing from his bag. He started asking everyone if they'd seen it. Eventually, someone discovered it lying under a bench, smashed to pieces.

Not surprisingly, everyone denied knowing anything about it, so the lad had to finish getting changed so he could take his complaint to the teacher.

Still, Ryan watched.

Jasper kept glancing over, wondering what Ryan had planned.

Just a few more minutes…

Troy finished getting dressed. As he pulled on his shoes, he screamed.

'What?' asked his mates, frozen in shock.

'My foot! There's something in my shoe.' Troy tried to take the shoe back off, and as he did it, he yelled again, his eyes watering with pain.

His grey school sock was stained dark with blood, and as Troy lifted his foot, a large triangle of broken glass stuck out the bottom.

'Fetch a teacher,' someone yelled.

Another lad knelt down and held Troy's foot by the ankle, so he didn't put it on the floor and push the glass in any further.

It only took a minute for the teacher to arrive. While they carried out first aid, Ryan finished getting changed. As he left the changing room, Jasper sidled up to him.

'Happy?' asked Ryan.

'It seems I underestimated you,' acknowledged Jasper. 'That was quality.'

'There's no way he's going to be playing in that match tomorrow now.'

'Where did you find the glass?' asked Jasper.

'The broken phone screen.'

Ryan had struggled at first to think of anything that he could break to put in Troy's shoes. Fortunately, most of the boys at St Oswalds had mobile phones in their bags, and breaking the screen had been easy.

'Looks like I owe you five hundred pounds,' said Jasper, like it was no big deal.

'And your respect,' pointed out Ryan.

That made Jasper laugh. 'You have that, Jacob. You definitely have that.'

26. MANSION

'Want to come back to my place?' asked Jasper, as they filed out of school.

Ryan couldn't believe it. 'Today? Won't your parents mind?'

'I don't have a mum and Dad won't be back until much later. He won't even know.'

Could this be any more perfect?

Ryan pulled out his phone. 'I'd better ask my mum.'

'Don't ask her. *Tell* her.'

'I will.'

Ryan fired off a text message, explaining that he was going to a friend's house. He sent it to 'Mum' in his contacts, knowing that it would go to a burner phone at the motorhome.

'Oh, there's one more thing.' Jasper snatched Ryan's phone out of his hand. 'You can't take this with you.'

'Why not?'

'My dad won't let anyone bring any tech in the house. Security is a big issue. Don't worry. Simon will look after it, won't you?' Jasper grabbed a lad by the shoulder, forcing him to spin around and face them. 'I'll give you twenty for your trouble.'

'I guess.' Simon took it from Jasper.

'I don't need to tell you what will happen if you break

that, do I?'

Simon slipped the phone into his blazer pocket. 'I'll be careful.'

'But what if my mum tries to phone?' asked Ryan.

'Just tell her it ran out of battery. You're not gonna go soft on me now, are you?'

Ryan shook his head. 'I don't see why I can't keep it.'

'It's a house rule.'

And suddenly you care about the rules, thought Ryan, but he stayed quiet. He wasn't about to risk his friendship with Jasper, just when he was about to get access to the Wolff house.

When they'd come up with the plan, they'd expected it would take a few days for Ryan to get close to Jasper. Even longer to get invited to his house. They'd never dreamed he'd be asked back on the first day.

Still, it hadn't been easy to win Jasper's friendship. He'd had to earn it the hard way, by smashing some kid's phone and filling a boy's shoes with glass.

The question was whether it would all be worth it in the end.

***

They got off at Jasper's stop.

It was the rich part of the city. Large houses were set back from the road. Jasper's was one of the biggest in the street.

'Nice place,' muttered Ryan. 'Your dad must be loaded. What does he do?'

'He runs a technology firm,' explained Jasper. 'They

make stuff for the army. That's why he's so paranoid about security.'

They entered through the front door into a spacious hallway. Jasper kicked off his shoes and dumped his bag. Ryan followed suit.

'Want a drink?' Jasper led him through to a huge kitchen-diner with a view out to the garden which was full of exotic plants.

'This place is amazing.'

'We have another house as well, out by the coast. But this is closer to school. Coke ok?'

'Great.'

Jasper poured two glasses and handed one to Ryan. 'Come on, I'll show you where the real action happens.'

He headed back to the hallway and opened a small door that Ryan had assumed was a cupboard. Instead, a staircase descended into the basement. Bright lights lit the way.

'We have a games room,' explained Jasper, 'and I think you'll like it.'

'Sounds good.' Ryan followed him down, an involuntary shiver running down his spine as the door slammed shut behind him.

At the bottom of the stairs, another door led through a massive underground space. A pool table, ping-pong table and games equipment were spread out between large pillars that held up the house above. The brick walls were painted black, but coloured LED strips bordered the ceiling, shifting gradually from red to blue to green to yellow, then back again. In the corner was a gaming area with sofas, a huge TV and a top-of-the-range console. Ryan walked towards it, checking out the pile of games on top.

'You got *Fields of War*?' he asked.

'I *love* that game,' said Jasper. 'We can play that soon. But first, I want to show you this.' He pointed to another doorway.

'What else you got hidden away?' asked Ryan, following him through.

Jasper's eyes gleamed. 'Something no-one else has. An experimental VR console.' He walked to the corner and held up a helmet. 'Wait until you see this.' He put down his drink and started fiddling with the buttons. 'I'll set it up and then you can have a go.'

'Ok. Sure.'

'It won't take a minute, but I have to navigate the menus and it's tricky if you've never done it.' He put on the helmet and got to work.

The room was almost empty, except for a large mesh chair. There was a TV screen on the wall, which showed some games menus. While Jasper was busy setting it up, Ryan sidled over to the table where the boy had left his drink. He slipped a sachet from his pocket and poured the powder into the glass, watching it dissolve in the dark liquid.

Everything was going to plan. It was almost too easy.

A few minutes later, Jasper took off the helmet. 'Ok, it's ready. Take a seat. You're gonna love this.'

Ryan dropped into the chair. 'Do you get to watch what I'm doing on the screen?'

'Yeah, the flattened version. But it's nothing like what you'll experience.'

Ryan took the headset and put it on. It covered his eyes and ears, only leaving his mouth and nose free.

But the moment it was on, he was transported somewhere else; he was in the cockpit of a plane that was in the middle of a dogfight. The graphics were incredible.

'How do the controls work?' he asked.

But he couldn't hear any response, only the noise of the simulation. It didn't matter. He soon worked it out. He could look at the controls and think about what he wanted to do, and his virtual hands obeyed. It was way beyond any kind of VR he'd played before.

Fighter planes came towards him, rockets launching in his direction. He swooped down, then up, shaking the heat-seekers off his tail.

Then he twisted and spun, locking one plane in his sights. He fired, blowing the plane out of the sky. He could almost feel the warmth of the blast from his own cockpit.

Something beeped and flashed. The word 'DANGER' appeared on his control panel. Ryan glanced around, trying to work out what the problem was.

He saw it too late. A plane right above him, descending at speed, opening fire.

The last thing he saw was the control panel explode.

The words 'Game Over' flashed before his eyes.

Jasper lifted off the helmet and Ryan was back in the basement, blinking in the bright light.

'Enjoy that?' asked Jasper, peering down at him. 'You looked like you were cacking yourself.'

'Pretty much,' admitted Ryan. He went to stand up,

but found he couldn't. His wrists and ankles had been strapped to the chair. Even his neck was held in place 'Hey, what gives?'

'Oh, that's meant to be for your safety,' explained Jasper, a thin smile forming on his lips. 'People can thrash around when they're immersed in the simulation.'

'Can you let me out?'

'No.' Jasper folded his arms.

'Why not?'

'Because I know who you really are.'

Ryan acted surprised. 'I don't know what you mean.'

'I think you do, Ryan.'

27. TRAP

Ryan tried not to panic. 'My name's not Ryan. It's Jacob.'

'Give it up. There's no point pretending.' Jasper paced around the room, a twisted look on his face. 'You're the boy who sabotaged my dad's latest project. He told me all about it. You cost us billions.'

'Yeah, like that matters.' Ryan struggled against the straps. 'You're still rich. Look at this place.'

'You must have thought you were so clever, coming to my school, pretending to be someone else. Do you think I'd really be friends with scum like you?'

Now he thought about it, it had been way too easy. Jasper had latched on to him the moment he saw him. You didn't make friends that quickly. Not with someone like Jasper. But then...

'You almost walked away from me. In the canteen.'

'I didn't want you getting suspicious. And I was curious to see how far you'd go to stay friends with me. It's interesting that you were willing to injure a total stranger just to get what you were after.'

'It wasn't like that,' said Ryan. But Jasper was right. He'd done exactly what he'd been mad at Three for in Blackfell. He'd allowed himself to be persuaded to cause someone else pain.

The boy smirked at him. 'What was the plan? Hold me to ransom? Try to get my dad to confess?'

'Your dad had me thrown into Blackfell. I need to clear my name.'

Jasper laughed. 'Well, that's not gonna happen. You're going straight back.'

'No, please.' Ryan was desperate. 'You don't know what they do to us.'

'Oh, but I do, Ryan.' Jasper leaned against the wall, swigging his Coke. His face was different now. Harder. Even in the ridiculous yellow and black striped blazer, he looked like a monster. 'My dad gave me access to some of the security footage. He knew how much I'd enjoy watching you suffer.' A wicked grin spread across Jasper's face. 'How long did it take you to finish scrubbing the dorm clean with a toothbrush?'

This was bad. This was really bad. Even if the powerful sedative acted fast, Ryan would still be strapped in the chair when Jasper awoke or Conrad returned. That wouldn't end well.

'You're sick, you know that? Your whole family is.'

'Maybe.' Jasper ran his hand through his long fringe. 'But I know one thing for sure. You're going to regret coming here.'

Ryan glared at him. 'Why? Because I have to look at your smug face?'

'No, because no-one can stop me from doing what I'm about to do.'

Jasper disappeared through the doorway. While he was gone, Ryan tried to wriggle free, but the straps held him fast. Seconds later, Jasper was back.

'Ever wanted a tattoo, Ryan?' The boy reached into a small leather case, pulling out a long metal needle which glinted in the spotlights.

Ryan could barely speak. 'No.'

'That's a shame, because you're about to get one. Right here on your forehead.' Jasper prodded his cold finger against Ryan's skin. 'Can you guess what it's going to be?'

'I don't know.'

'I'll give you a clue. Only boys have them.'

Ryan swore. 'Not that. Anything but that.'

'Don't worry, Ryan.' Jasper stroked his hair, like he was some sort of pet. 'I'm sure you'll be able to get it removed eventually, when you're released from Blackfell. You'll only have to put up with it for a few years.'

'Please, Jasper. Don't do it.'

'Do you know how pathetic you sound? I haven't even started yet. Now, hold still. I'm afraid this *is* going to hurt.'

Ryan cried out as Jasper started on the tattoo. He could feel the needle being pushed into his forehead.

Jasper sniggered at Ryan's discomfort. 'I hope it doesn't get too badly infected. I've never done one of these before. And I'm not what you'd call a great artist.'

Ryan blinked back tears as the boy continued his torture, stabbing his forehead again and again. The worst part wasn't the immediate pain. It was the knowledge that from now on, his face would be ruined. People would laugh at him. Or pity him. He didn't know which would be worse.

'I hope you weren't ever hoping to have a girlfriend,' mocked Jasper. He took a step back as if to admire his work, then picked up his drink.

'Is—is—is it finished?' asked Ryan.

Jasper almost choked. 'No. This is going to take hours. But it is *so* worth it.'

'Your dad won't like it,' argued Ryan, desperate to change the boy's mind. 'He won't want to be implicated in this kind of abuse.'

'Whatever.' Jasper yawned, as though Ryan was boring him. 'Dad can get mad if he wants. No-one can prove it happened here.'

Ryan was desperate. He yelled out, but Jasper grabbed hold of his throat. 'Want me to tape your mouth shut?'

'No.'

'Then keep quiet.'

Jasper put down his drink and picked up the needle. 'Time to get back to work.'

Ryan blinked back tears as Jasper pressed on, every sharp prick bringing him closer to humiliation.

When Ryan had come up with a plan to clear his name, he knew it had risks, but he never expected he'd wind up in a basement being scarred for life by a crazy psychopath. He should have taken the offer of staying off grid. Now, he'd be sent back to Blackfell, but it would be even worse than before. Even when they released him, he'd have something repulsive on his forehead.

Surely the sedative would take effect soon?

But Jasper hadn't finished his drink. Maybe he hadn't taken enough?

There were ten more minutes of intense pain before something changed: Jasper staggered backwards and dropped the needle. The boy who had looked so confident, so evil, seemed confused.

'What—What's happening?' He sat down hard on the floor, unable to regain his balance. 'What did you do?'

Ryan stared back at him. 'Let me go and I'll tell you.'

Jasper locked eyes with him, then glanced over at his drink as realisation hit. 'You drugged me. My Coke.'

'If you unstrap me, I can make sure it's not fatal. Otherwise, I'll just watch you die.'

The boy's eyes narrowed. 'You're bluffing. You didn't mean to kill me, just knock me out.'

'Maybe. Maybe not. But is it worth the risk?'

Jasper was lying on the floor now, barely able to speak. 'You'll still be here… when I wake up. And then I'll… finish what I started.'

The boy couldn't fight the tiredness. His eyes closed.

His enemy might be unconscious, but Ryan wasn't going anywhere. When he'd put the powder in Jasper's drink, he'd assumed that the kid would pass out and he'd be able to do what he liked in the house. Instead, he was strapped to the chair, unable to move.

He kept working at the straps, but they were strong and tight.

There was nothing he could do but wait.

***

'Look who it is.'

Ryan came to with a start.

At some point, he'd drifted off. The adrenaline had worn him out, and his body needed to recover.

Conrad Wolff stood over him. 'Ryan Jacobs, right here in my house. Who would have believed it?'

Wolff was a genius inventor and entrepreneur. He was also corrupt to the core, and had thought nothing of killing innocent people.

'Let me go.' Ryan spat out the words, furious to be discovered strapped to a chair.

'I don't think you're in any place to make demands, do you? You drugged my son.'

Ryan looked down at Jasper, who was lying on the floor, now in the recovery position. 'He was torturing me; trying to tattoo my forehead.'

Wolff laughed at that. 'I can't blame him. What was the plan, Ryan?'

Ryan glared at him. 'I'm not telling you.'

Wolff walked up to the chair and felt around in Ryan's pockets. With a look of triumph, he removed a small recording device. 'Really? This? You were hoping I'd say something incriminating?'

'Maybe.' Ryan looked away, embarrassed.

'It's not the only one, is it? I seem to remember we've played this game before.' Wolff lifted Ryan's trouser legs and checked his socks. Another small device was tucked inside one. 'I trust that's everything? If not, be assured that you will be searched before you go anywhere. There's no way you're getting out of here with any kind of device. And in case you're wondering, the walls of this house block all transmissions.'

'Then let me go.'

'You expect to walk out? Not a chance. You'll be sent back to Blackfell. The only question is whether I let Jasper finish his artwork first.'

Ryan gulped.

Wolff enjoyed watching him squirm. 'There's something else I need to tell you, Ryan, now this rather unique opportunity has presented itself.'

'What?'

'I changed my mind about dropping the charges against your beloved Mr Davids. He's still being held on conspiracy to commit an act of terror.'

'But we had a deal!' Ryan strained against the straps, his blood boiling. 'You said if I confessed, you'd let him and the others go.'

'Dear Lionel was too dangerous. Safer to have him behind bars.'

'You lied.' Ryan spat at Wolff, the only way he could express his defiance.

Wolff took a handkerchief out of his waistcoat pocket and wiped the saliva from his face. 'Now, now, Ryan, you don't want to upset me. Not when I am such a close friend of the governor at Blackfell.'

Ryan was desperate to score points against Wolff. 'You're just angry because I won. I sneaked the antivirus into your system and stopped the shutdown. And I foiled your plan to sucker the military into paying for unnecessary upgrades.'

'That's true, Ryan, but here's the thing. Only you and I know that. Everyone else thinks *you* caused the shutdown, and *I* stopped it. Even your friends don't believe you. So, who really won? Do you think you'll feel victorious when you're back in your cell?'

Wolff was right. Ryan didn't feel like a winner, and his enemy had all the power.

'Don't send me back,' pleaded Ryan. 'I'll do anything you want. Anything.'

Conrad tilted his head to the side. 'Will you tell me who helped you escape?'

Ryan wasn't sure whether it would matter. The Outlier was already implicated in so many crimes that one more wouldn't make a difference. But even to say Sam's name felt like an act of betrayal.

He shook his head. 'I can't.'

'Then I hope the governor isn't too mad that you got away from his precious facility. I don't think that's ever happened before.'

'Screw the governor.'

Wolff held up the small recording device. 'Want to say that again? I'm sure he'd love to hear it?'

Ryan bit his tongue. Wolff was about to send him into the lion's den. There was no point making it worse.

'No? I thought not.'

Jasper stirred on the floor.

Conrad knelt down next to him. 'It's ok, son. I'm here.'

The boy rubbed his eyes and propped himself up on his elbows. He saw Ryan in front of him, still strapped to the chair. 'He tried to sneak in here, then he drugged me.'

'I know.' Conrad helped him to his feet. 'Let's get you somewhere comfortable.'

Jasper narrowed his eyes at Ryan. 'This isn't over.'

'He's right,' said Conrad. 'Don't go anywhere, will you

166

now?'

As they made their way out of the basement, they left Ryan in the chair, with no hope of escape.

He'd walked right into Jasper's trap.

And now, he would pay.

28. WAIT

They weren't in any hurry.

Ryan sat in the dark for hours, drifting in and out of sleep as the night wore on. He'd considered yelling for help, but he knew it would only attract the wrong sort of attention, and he wasn't in any hurry for Jasper to resume work on the tattoo.

When the lights came on, he guessed it must be morning. Jasper came down the steps and Ryan sat up, suddenly awake.

'How's my new friend doing?' sneered Jasper. He was dressed for school. 'Not too bored down here, I hope?'

'If you let me out now, I won't say anything about what you've done,' said Ryan. 'I'll just run away.'

Jasper laughed. 'That's cute. *You're* threatening *me*.'

'I'm offering you a deal.'

'No deals, Ryan. I've got some work to finish on your forehead. But, sadly, Father says that education must come first, so that has to wait until I'm back from school. You can stay here.'

Another seven hours sat in the chair. It wasn't a pleasant thought.

'I need the toilet.' Ryan wasn't kidding.

'Excellent. I'll enjoy the thought of you sitting in your

own mess. Later, Ryan.'

With that, Jasper headed out of the basement, switching off the lights as he went.

***

Darkness.

Ryan squirmed, trying to ignore the smell coming from his trousers. He wondered how long he'd sat there, and how much longer it would be.

Bad as it was, he knew the worse was still to come. All he had to look forward to was more pain as Jasper finished the tattoo, and then the horrific future that awaited him when he returned to Blackfell.

Way to go, Ryan.

He'd properly screwed this up, even by his standards. Sitting here, he couldn't believe he'd ever thought the plan would succeed.

It could still work…

No, he was kidding himself, clinging on to hope. When they'd come up with it, they had no idea that Jasper would recognise Ryan, and now everything had gone wrong. If Jasper had seen footage from Blackfell, he'd probably spot Three a mile off. Their plan was ruined.

It was best to face facts, however grim the reality. Ryan was going to spend the rest of his childhood at Blackfell. And without Three there, someone else would rise to the top of the food chain and the governor would ensure that they were rewarded for making his life a misery.

He tried to stop thinking about it. But there was nothing else to do, nothing to distract him from his fear.

***

BANG!

An almighty commotion.

Heavy boots on the stairs.

Lights switched on.

Soldiers in tactical gear stormed into the basement, guns sweeping the room.

'Clear,' shouted one, from the games area next door.

'Clear,' shouted another.

The soldier standing in front of Ryan lowered his weapon and raised his radio to his ear. 'Sir, you're never gonna believe this. You better come and check this out.'

There was nothing but static in reply. Conrad Wolff hadn't been kidding about the house blocking all transmissions.

The soldier's message had to be relayed by the others in the unit, making its way up the line of command.

'Please let me out,' begged Ryan, as the soldier awaited his superior.

The man hesitated, unsure what to do. 'Sorry, lad, you'll have to wait.'

This time, it wasn't for long.

There were footsteps on the stairs and the soldier stiffened. A man swept into the room, dressed in black combats. Ryan recognised him immediately: it was Special Agent Hawkings, the agent who had led the investigation into the shutdown. It was Hawkings who Ryan had given a false confession to when Wolff threatened his friends.

For a moment, Ryan stared at him and he stared back.

The man broke the silence. 'In trouble again, Jacobs?'

'Maybe.' Ryan wasn't sure what the agent knew.

'The last I heard, you were on your way to Blackfell. Instead, you're in Conrad Wolff's house, strapped to a chair.'

'I fancied a holiday.'

That made Hawkings laugh. He made his way over and started undoing the leather straps. 'Care to explain how you did it?'

'How I did what?'

'Escaped Blackfell. Then got evidence that Conrad Wolff framed you.'

He'd heard the recording then. The plan had worked!

Ryan shrugged. 'Does it matter?'

'Maybe not.' Hawkings undid the last strap and Ryan stood up, relieved to be free of the chair. Hawkings swore and held his nose. 'You stink, Jacobs.'

'I might need a change of underwear.'

Hawkings turned to the soldier. 'Get Jacobs some clean clothes. There should be some in one of the bedrooms upstairs. Wolff has a son the same age.'

The soldier hurried off.

Only one question mattered to Ryan. 'What happens now?'

'Conrad Wolff has some explaining to do.'

171

'I meant, to me. Will you send me back to Blackfell?'

Hawkings shook his head. 'Hell, no. From what I can tell from the recording I just listened to, you should never have gone there in the first place.'

Ryan felt like a ten-tonne weight had been lifted from his shoulders. 'I get to go home?'

'Devonmoor Academy, if that counts?'

Ryan grinned. 'It'll do.' Truthfully, he couldn't wait to get back.

Hawkings put his hands on his hips. 'I still want to know how you did it. How did you get a recording of Wolff admitting to the crimes, while they had you strapped to a chair in his basement?'

'First, I want an apology. You locked me up, and I was innocent.'

Hawkings frowned. 'It was your own fault you got sent to Blackfell. You confessed to causing the shutdown.'

'Yeah, but if you'd been any good at your job, you'd have known that wasn't true.'

The agent rolled his eyes. 'Fine. I'm sorry you got the blame. Now, will you tell me how you did it?'

'I planted a recording device in Jasper's top blazer pocket. It was tiny. I figured he wouldn't notice. I knew they'd check me for devices, but they weren't likely to check Jasper's clothes.'

'Clever,' said Hawkings. 'But how did you get it back? You were strapped to a chair.'

'I had help,' admitted Ryan. 'A friend of mine. He caught the bus the next morning. It was all part of the plan. He'd get in a fight with Jasper and during the scuffle, he'd remove the bug. Then he'd send the contents to the authorities.'

'I don't suppose you'll tell me your friend's name?'

Ryan shook his head.

Agent Hawkings sighed. 'I thought not. Ok, come on. Let's get you cleaned up.'

***

Hawkings didn't ask any more questions as they made their way upstairs. He ushered Ryan into a luxurious bathroom and told him to take a shower.

Ryan didn't need telling twice.

First, though, he checked out his face in the mirror, desperate to see the damage Jasper had inflicted.

It could have been worse. The boy hadn't been exaggerating when he'd said the tattoo would take hours. So far, all he'd done was carved a bendy line into Ryan's forehead. It looked like a weird scar, nothing more. Given what Ryan had imagined it might look like, it was a huge relief.

Ryan stripped off and stepped into the shower. He almost fell asleep under the jets of steaming water, only shutting off the water when a soldier banged on the door to hurry him along.

They gave him some of Jasper's clothes: a designer tracksuit, a polo shirt and some underwear. It all felt smooth and comfortable, nothing like the harsh clothing of Blackfell or the itchy uniform of St Oswalds.

When Ryan emerged, he felt like a different boy. He was no longer a prisoner, of Jasper Wolff or of Blackfell.

Against all odds, his crazy plan had worked.

Conrad Wolff might have searched him for secret recording devices and discovered everything he had, but he never searched his own son.

There were so many things that could have gone wrong. Jasper or Conrad could have found the device. Or the boy might have removed his blazer. Or Conrad might have kept his mouth shut.

But, Ryan had pulled it off, with the help of his newfound friends.

He wondered if he would ever see Three and the Outlier again, now he was to be taken back to Devonmoor.

But, somehow, he knew he would.

29. TRUTH

'I told you Ryan was innocent,' insisted Lady Devonmoor, taking a sip of her tea. 'I knew he'd never do anything like that.'

The colonel snorted. 'I didn't find it that hard to believe.'

'To be fair, Julius, you've never liked the boy.'

The colonel grunted.

Ryan sat in the armchair opposite, relieved to be back in the familiar surroundings of the academy. He had been taken to the headteacher's office as soon as he'd arrived. Colonel Keller and Dr Torren had been summoned as well, but even being in a room with the colonel didn't dampen his spirits.

Ryan was glad to hear that Lady Devonmoor had always known he wasn't responsible for the shutdown, but that also confused him.

'If you knew I was innocent, why did you let them drag me off to Blackfell?' he asked.

The colonel smirked. It was clear why *he'd* let it happen.

'The evidence was too compelling,' explained the doctor. 'We had our suspicions that they had forced you to confess, but we couldn't prove it. And Hawkings wouldn't let us meet with you while the investigation was underway to clarify what had happened.'

So, when Ryan had been stuck in the hospital, they hadn't been ignoring him; they'd been forbidden from visiting.

'But, sir, what about Mr Davids? Has he been released yet? You must have known *he* was innocent.'

Dr Torren nodded. 'Mr Davids is on his way back here, thanks to you. It was noble that you tried to take the bullet for him with your false confession.'

'It didn't work though,' said Ryan, bitterly.

Lady Devonmoor leaned forward and gave him a warm smile. 'You tried, Ryan. That's what matters. You did what you could to save your friends. That's true bravery.'

'Try telling them that,' said Ryan. 'All my friends think I caused the shutdown, and because of that, they think I killed Jael and the others.'

'We've already set the record straight,' soothed Lady Devonmoor. 'We called a special assembly today to inform all the cadets of how you'd been framed. Everyone knows the truth.'

That cheered Ryan up.

'Can I see them?' he asked.

'Not until you get out of those civilian clothes and back into your uniform,' snapped the colonel, looking down at Ryan's tracksuit with disgust.

'Yes, sir.'

'Well?' The colonel stood over him. 'What are you waiting for, cadet?'

'Right now?'

'Yes, right now. MOVE IT!'

Ryan stood up and edged towards the door, stopping just before he stepped out. 'Lady Devonmoor?'

'Yes, Ryan?'

'Thanks for believing in me.'

Lady Devonmoor's eyes twinkled. 'Thank you, dear, for proving me right.'

***

The dorm was empty; it was evening and the other boys would be in the common room. He'd join them as soon as he'd changed.

Ryan would much rather have carried on wearing the designer tracksuit, but he stripped everything off and pulled on the standard Devonmoor uniform that was folded in the wardrobe.

White vest.

Grey trousers and jacket, a thin maroon stripe down each side.

Stupidly long grey socks that folded at the knee.

Shiny black boots.

In terms of style, it wasn't much better than what he'd had to wear at Blackfell, but at least it was clean.

After checking himself in the mirror, and sweeping his hair down over the curved scar Jasper had left on his forehead, Ryan raced upstairs.

He burst into the common room, desperate to see his friends. The room stretched above the dorms, with sloping ceilings and large wooden rafters. Sofas nestled between the beams, consoles bleeped and at the far end was a dartboard and a pool table. It was the only place in the academy where cadets could relax.

The hubbub and laughter died away as soon as everyone saw Ryan, and he hesitated in the doorway, unsure what they were thinking.

An awkward pause.

'Look who's back.' Kev walked over, a pool cue in hand. 'If it isn't Ryan Jacobs, the troublemaker.'

Ryan looked the taller lad in the eye, wondering whether Kev still hated him. Lady Devonmoor might have tried to explain everything to the cadets, but that didn't mean they'd believed her.

'You know I'm innocent, right? You know I didn't kill Jael and the others?'

The room was deadly silent, the cadets waiting for the drama to play out.

Kev was a natural leader and an athlete. Everyone liked him. If Kev wanted to beat Ryan up, he'd have no difficulty doing it. And no-one would stop him.

Still, Ryan stood his ground. He wouldn't flinch and he sure as hell wasn't going to flee. If Kev wanted to punch him, he'd take it on the chin.

He needn't have worried. The older lad grabbed him by the shoulders and pulled him in for a hug. 'You stupid idiot. Why did you confess to something you didn't do? We thought we'd lost you as well.'

Ryan's best friend, Lee, flung himself at them both, making it into more of a group hug, while everyone else clapped and cheered.

'Seems like you're something of a hero, Ryan,' said Lee.

'Makes a pleasant change,' muttered Ryan. He tried

to look like he didn't care about the applause, but even he was blinking back tears.

When he pulled away, he saw Sparks standing nearby, looking ashamed. 'I'm sorry I doubted you, Ryan. I should have known you weren't guilty.'

'It's ok. Even I started to think I was.' Ryan grinned and hugged the overweight cadet.

'What was Blackfell like?' asked Lee. 'Is it as bad as they say?'

'Worse,' said Ryan. 'It's hell.'

'Then you better hope you never have to go back there.'

The voice was cold, threatening. Ryan turned to see James Sarrell standing behind him, his face twisted in a permanent scowl. At seventeen, Sarrell was much older than Ryan. He was also an expert in martial arts and a bully. Nothing gave him more pleasure than getting Ryan in trouble.

'Lay off, Sarrell. I've dealt with much worse than you.'

'Yeah? Aren't you forgetting something?'

Sarrell gave Ryan a meaningful look. Ryan knew exactly what he was talking about. Just before they had taken him to Blackfell, Sarrell had found out about the StealthBot, a secret project that Ryan and Sparks had worked on together. At one point, the robot had run amok, almost killing students and teachers at the school. No-one ever found out they were responsible except Sarrell, and he was using it to blackmail Ryan.

'I expect to see you in the gym for your next boxing lesson on Wednesday night. Don't be late.' Sarrell ruffled Ryan's hair, then walked away.

'I never understood why you let him use you as a punchbag,' said Kev. 'You planning to keep doing that?'

'I guess,' admitted Ryan. Sarrell's boxing lessons were not something he looked forward to. Last time, he'd been beaten to a pulp. But what could he do? If Sarrell told anyone about the StealthBot, both he and Sparks would be in serious trouble. He couldn't risk doing anything that might land him back at Blackfell.

'Actually, Ryan, you might not need to,' said Sparks. 'While you've been away, I've been working on a plan to solve our little problem with Sarrell. I'll tell you about it later.'

Ryan smiled. 'Can't wait.'

'Tell us more about Blackfell,' urged Lee.

He wasn't the only one who was interested. Cadets crowded around the sofa where Ryan sat, desperate to hear what it was like.

'It's like a boot camp. But it's worse. The governor does stuff that has to be illegal. You share a dorm with some other lads, and they had bribed the boys in my room to bully me...'

Ryan tried to explain what he'd been through, but the more he tried, the harder he found it. Words didn't do it justice. No-one would believe how harsh the place had been. That was probably how the governor got away with it. He couldn't describe how it had made him feel, the dark scar it had left on his soul.

'How did you escape?' asked Lee.

'I hacked the security system. There was a keypad in the room and I prised it open and hot-wired it. Once I got to a computer in the office, I was home free.' He felt guilty about lying to his friends, but he didn't want to say anything about the Outlier. It wouldn't be a great idea to admit he was now friends with the number one enemy of Devonmoor Academy.

Ranjit Jeet raised his eyebrows. 'And you just walked out?'

'Well, I ran.' Ryan looked away, his face turning red. 'Blackfell is in the middle of woods and moorland, so once you get out, it's easy to hide. They don't have enough guards to search everywhere.'

Ranjit didn't look convinced. As one of Dr Torren's best students, he knew Ryan was lying. But the others were lapping it up and Ranjit didn't have a chance to challenge him further.

'You're something else, you know that?' grinned Kev. 'I never thought you'd make it back.'

Ryan felt something welling up inside him as he looked around at his friends. 'You know what? Neither did I.'

30. COFFEE

Ryan was in heaven as he tucked into his lunch in the school canteen. He'd never complain about the food at Devonmoor again. So what if you only got decent food if you did well in the canteen test? At least you got something.

And today he'd done well. He'd bagged himself some chicken wraps and a raspberry trifle. It was the best meal he'd had for ages.

He'd just about finished when a shadow fell over the table. He knew who it was before he turned around.

'Hi, Sarrell,' he said, as if he didn't care.

'I am still a prefect, Jacobs, so you address me as *sir.*'

'Hi, Sarrell, *sir.*' Ryan gave him a mischievous smile which was bound to wind him up.

'I forgot how much I enjoyed having you around until today. It's going to be fun to get you back in the ring. So much fun that I've decided I can't wait until Wednesday. You have an extra boxing lesson tonight.'

'But it's Saturday.'

'And?' Sarrell gave an evil grin. 'It's not like you have a choice, is it Jacobs. Seven-thirty. Don't be late.'

Ryan downed the rest of his drink, then stood up and burped in Sarrell's face. 'Screw you.'

The bully raised his eyebrows. 'You sure you want to risk it, Jacobs?'

'I'm not showing up to any more of your boxing sessions, and I'm not scared of your stupid threats. So, do your worst, Sarrell, *sir*.'

'You'll regret this.' The prefect scowled, turned on his heels and marched away.

Ryan sat down and glanced over at Sparks, who sat opposite. 'This plan of yours had better work.'

'Oh, don't worry. It will.'

At that moment, Ayana ran up to them, an excited look on her face. 'Guess who just got back!'

Ryan's eyes widened. 'Mr Davids?'

Ayana nodded. 'I saw him in the corridor.'

Ryan cleared his tray as fast as he could, then dashed down the stairs. He knew where his favourite teacher would be. As he burst through the doors of the computer lab, Mr Davids was standing there, a smile on his face.

'Ah, Ryan, my boy, I believe I need to say thank you, yes?' The teacher pushed his glasses up his nose. 'If it wasn't for you, I think I would still be in prison.'

Ryan shrugged like it was no big deal. 'We both got falsely accused, but now we're free. That's all that matters.' He stepped forward and hugged the teacher, who looked surprised that a student would ever do that.

'I'm not sure we're supposed to... oh well, in the circumstances.' Mr Davids patted him on the back and stepped away. 'How did you clear our names?'

'I did what I had to do. I got Wolff to confess.'

'That can't have been easy. He's a clever man.'

That was high praise indeed from Mr Davids, but Ryan knew it was true. Conrad Wolff had almost outsmarted them both.

'I hope he rots in whatever jail they throw him in. He deserves to pay.'

Mr Davids gave Ryan a sad look. 'Don't let your anger destroy you, my boy. We have to move on, yes? Don't let ourselves become bitter. That's what causes wars and conflict. Better to forgive and forget.'

'Maybe.' Ryan wasn't going to argue with the teacher and spoil the special moment, but he wanted Wolff to suffer. For years.

The door to the lab opened and Sarah Devonmoor walked in.

'Ah, Sarah,' said the teacher.

The prefect allowed herself a smile. 'It's good to have you back, sir. We all knew you were innocent.'

'Thank you, my girl. We have a lot to catch up on.'

'Yes, but first I'm afraid Jacobs has to report to the colonel.' She turned to Ryan and gave a scowl. 'It looks like you're already in trouble. He's demanding to meet you and Sparks in the engineering block.'

'I'm sure it's all just a misunderstanding,' said Ryan. 'We'll soon have it all cleared up.'

'I'm not sure, Jacobs. He sounded furious.'

'He always sounds furious.'

'Either way, you need to get a move on.'

'Catch you later, sir,' said Ryan, backing out of the lab. As he made his way over to the engineering block, he hoped Sparks knew what he was doing.

If not, they'd both be in a lot of trouble.

***

Sparks was already there.

He was standing to attention, the colonel towering in front of him. Sarrell stood nearby, looking victorious.

Ryan took his place next to his friend, then saluted the colonel.

'Let's not pretend you're playing by the rules, Jacobs,' sneered the teacher. 'You've been back for less than twenty-four hours and I'm already getting reports that you boys were responsible for the attack on the school last term.'

'I know nothing about that, sir,' said Ryan.

'Denial. Hardly an unexpected response.' The colonel turned to Sarrell. 'Well, where's this killer robot they created?'

'They keep it over here.' Sarrell walked over to the far corner, with the boys and the colonel close behind. 'Unless they've hidden it. They probably have.'

He pulled back a tarpaulin in the corner, and was just as surprised as Ryan to find the StealthBot lying there, exactly as they'd left it.

With its sleek black armour plating and single red eye it looked just as dangerous as Ryan knew it was.

What was Sparks thinking? Now Sarrell and the colonel had all the evidence they needed to get them expelled.

'I see. You boys want to explain yourselves?'

Ryan looked at Sparks. He didn't know what to say.

The fat kid smiled at the colonel. 'Oh, that! That's just

Hughie.'

'I don't care what you call it, cadet. It's still a dangerous invention that wreaked havoc on this academy!'

'But, it's not,' protested Sparks. 'He's harmless.'

'Yeah, well why don't you turn him on,' suggested Sarrell, a gleam in his eye.

Sparks shuffled his feet. 'I wouldn't recommend that. He's not quite, err, perfected yet.'

'As I thought,' sneered Sarrell. 'It's too dangerous.'

'Is he right?' demanded the colonel.

'No, sir. Hughie wouldn't hurt a fly.'

'Then turn it on and prove it. That's an order.'

'If you insist,' sighed Sparks. He reached to the back of the StealthBot's neck and flipped a switch.

Ryan almost shouted out to stop him. It wasn't worth the risk. Last time this robot had been operational, it had threatened to assassinate anything that moved. One arm concealed a laser and the other a machine gun, though looking at it now, Ryan couldn't see evidence of either.

The eye began to glow, and the robot climbed to its feet. In this very lab, Ryan had faced this monster, and it had nearly destroyed him.

He wondered if that was about to happen again. He waited to hear those fatal words: 'THREAT DETECTED.' That's what the robot said, just before it started shooting.

But Sparks didn't appear worried.

'Afternoon, Hughie,' he said, cheerfully.

'Good afternoon, Master Sparks,' said the

StealthBot. Its voice was no longer harsh and robotic, but sing-song and friendly. 'How can I assist you today?'

'These people wanted to meet you,' explained Sparks. 'Can you tell them what you do?'

'I can do a large variety of tasks to assist people,' said the robot. 'Would you like a cup of coffee?'

'Does it have weapons?' said the colonel.

'No, it's not designed to hurt people,' insisted Sparks. 'It's like a butler, but stronger. I planned to use it in the lab to help me build things, when I need heavy things lifting. Stuff like that.'

'Allow me,' said the StealthBot, ignoring what they were saying. It reached into its side and pulled out a paper cup which it held in front of its stomach. A stream of hot black liquid squirted from its chest, missing the cup and soaking the colonel's trousers.

'Make it stop!' he ordered, jumping back, out of the way.

'No more coffee, Hughie,' said Sparks.

The stream of liquid stopped.

'Would you like milk?' asked the StealthBot. Before they could answer, it sprayed milk at the cup, most of it missing the target.

The colonel cursed. 'Switch that thing off, RIGHT NOW!'

Sparks shrugged and flipped the switch on the StealthBot's neck. The red eye stopped glowing, and the robot stood silently, an empty paper cup still in its hand.

'Like I said,' said Sparks, apologetically. 'It's still not finished. Sorry about the coffee, sir.'

The colonel glanced down at his stained trousers, then turned his fury on Sarrell. 'You seriously want me to believe that stupid contraption is responsible for the Code Zero incident? The only thing less intelligent than that machine is *you*. Don't you dare waste my time with any more of this nonsense.'

With that, the colonel strode from the engineering block, leaving the boys alone with Sarrell.

'Clever,' hissed Sarrell. 'You reprogrammed it and made a few changes. I see you took its weapons away.'

'What weapons?' asked Sparks, innocently. 'I think you must be mistaken.'

Sarrell was not convinced. 'I know what I saw, and I know what this is. And you're both going to pay. You mark my words.'

Ryan snorted. 'Well, I'm not going to be attending any more of your boxing classes, if it's all the same to you.'

'Boxing will be the last of your worries, Jacobs.' Leaving the threat hanging in the air, Sarrell marched off after the colonel.

'What do you think he'll do?' asked Sparks.

'Dunno. He doesn't know either, yet. But whatever it is, it can't be worse than having him belt me round the head repeatedly in the boxing ring.'

'I thought you were going to wet yourself when I turned Hughie on,' said Sparks.

'Yeah, well, it wouldn't be the first time. How did you reprogram it without me here?'

'I can do some basic programming,' insisted Sparks, looking offended.

'So, was that thing with the coffee all part of the plan,'

asked Ryan, 'or was that an error?'

'I'd prefer not to answer that.' Sparks slapped the robot on the back. 'Either way, I think we can agree Hughie did well.'

'*You* did well, Sparks,' insisted Ryan.

The fat boy beamed. 'I guess I did.'

31. BOOTS

Ryan knocked on Dr Torren's door.

'Come in.'

He entered the strange black room, which felt way too modern to be in a building this old. A floor-to-ceiling window made up the wall at the far end, overlooking the beautiful front gardens of the academy.

The room was empty except for two comfortable leather armchairs that faced each other. Dr Torren was in one of them, dressed in his three-piece suit.

'You asked to see me, sir.'

'I'm worried about you.'

Ryan hovered near the doorway. 'I'm fine.'

'Take a seat, Jacobs.'

Reluctantly, Ryan dropped into the chair.

Dr Torren watched him carefully, analysing every tiny movement, every subtle tell. 'You don't seem happy, since you got back,' he observed.

'But I am.'

'You're doing a good job of fooling everyone else. But I can see that something is wrong.'

Ryan sighed. 'I guess it's taking me a while to get over Blackfell. That's all. But it's only been a week. It'll get easier with time.'

The doctor nodded. 'That's quite a scar you've got on

your forehead.'

'It could have been worse.'

'Still, it must have been painful.'

Ryan stayed silent. He didn't care about that.

'Something else has changed about you since you were last at Devonmoor.' It wasn't a question.

'If you say so.' Ryan's body tensed.

'You're worried about something.'

Ryan shifted uncomfortably in his seat. 'I'm out of Blackfell. They've arrested Conrad Wolff. I've even dealt with an ongoing issue with Sarrell. For once, I don't have anything to be stressed about.'

That wasn't quite true. Ryan knew the Outlier was expecting him to find the Fractal Processor, and he had no idea how to do that. And there was no way he wanted to betray Mr Davids and the academy. But he couldn't tell Dr Torren any of that. Besides, if he was honest, that wasn't the only thing that was keeping him awake at night.

The doctor stayed quiet for a moment. 'It must be good to be back with your friends,' he suggested.

Ryan relaxed. This was much safer territory. 'Yeah. I missed them in Blackfell. And everyone is treating me like a hero since I got back.'

'Are you a hero?' asked the doctor.

'No.' Ryan said it more forcefully than he intended. 'I mean, of course not.' He hesitated. 'I did some things I'm not proud of. But it wasn't like I had a choice.'

'And yet…' The doctor looked at him, the pale blue eyes piercing Ryan's soul.

'Like I say, I did what had to be done.'

'You feel guilty about what you did.'

'Not at all,' shot back Ryan. 'They deserved it.'

'They?' enquired the doctor.

'The governor of Blackfell. Conrad and Jasper Wolff.'

Dr Torren raised his eyebrows. 'You really hate them.'

'Yes, I hate them. They're twisted and evil, and they made my life a living hell.'

'Hatred is a dark emotion. It can turn us into the things we despise.'

'I'm nothing like them,' spat Ryan. But tears pricked the corners of his eyes. 'They're psychopaths. They enjoy torturing people. I don't.' He flinched as he said it.

'Everyone enjoys feeling powerful,' said the doctor, his voice neutral. 'It's not the same.'

'Too right it's not.' Ryan forced himself to calm down. It was never a good idea to get emotional in front of the doctor.

'Take your boots off, Ryan.'

'Sir?'

'Your boots. Remove them.'

Ryan leaned forward and unlaced the combat boots. He pulled them off, revealing the thick grey socks underneath.

'Comfortable?' asked the doctor.

'I guess.'

'I always like that moment when you take off your shoes at the end of the day, you know what I mean?' Dr Torren smiled. 'It's like you can finally relax.'

'Are you trying to hypnotise me, sir?'

'No, I'm just making a point. Sometimes I wonder why

192

we do it. Why we wear shoes in the first place.'

Ryan remembered how painful it had been to wander through the forest in his socks. 'To protect our feet.'

Dr Torren leaned forwards. 'Exactly. Our hearts and minds are like that, too. We can't leave them exposed to every danger. Sometimes, we have to cover them up, to shield them with our tough exterior. It's ok to do that, as long as we don't do it all the time.'

Ryan stared out of the window. It looked like paradise out there: neat lawns and pretty flowers; blue skies and bright sunlight. But inside he felt cold. 'What if there's nothing soft to protect?'

A moment of silence, as they both thought about that.

Eventually, the doctor spoke. 'You see them, don't you? Those people you hate. Whenever you close your eyes.'

'Every time I look in the mirror,' admitted Ryan.

'You're not the same as them.'

'How do you know?' exploded Ryan. He stood up and walked over to the window, his back to the doctor. 'How can you be sure? When I tried to escape from Blackfell, I got to torture the governor. And you know what? I enjoyed it. And if I could do it again, I would.'

'It doesn't make you a monster.'

'So you say.'

'I mean it, Ryan.'

Ryan didn't respond.

The doctor pressed on. 'Do you know the difference between you and them?'

Ryan hesitated. He didn't. That was what troubled him. 'No,' he mumbled, ashamed to admit it.

'You don't *want* to be that kind of person. You're scared of yourself and what you're becoming. But that fear defines you. It's what makes you human. It keeps you soft. You need to listen to it, to let it become larger than your hatred.'

In a strange way, that made sense. Ryan didn't want to silence his better emotions. He wanted to care, and love, and to do the right thing. He turned to face the doctor. 'So, I'm not evil?'

Dr Torren smiled. 'Not even close. But, if I were you, I wouldn't ask Colonel Keller for his opinion on that.'

Ryan gave a weak smile. 'Thanks for the chat, sir. I already feel a lot better.'

'You can go now, if you like. But I'm always here if you want to talk.'

'I appreciate that.' Ryan headed for the door, grabbing his boots on the way.

'Aren't you going to put those on?' asked Dr Torren.

'Not yet,' said Ryan. 'First, there's something I need to do.'

EPILOGUE

There wasn't a cloud in the sky as Ryan made his way along the path. The academy grounds were peaceful. He could hear the birdsong, the gentle rustle of leaves overhead. He was still carrying his boots, and he enjoyed the feel of the soft grass underfoot.

Around the side of the main building, hidden at the far corner of the ornamental lawn was a crumbling brick wall. A rusty gate led through to a small orchard. Ryan hadn't been here much before; only to explore.

This part of the school was special: the garden of remembrance.

He didn't have to go far to find what he was after. Three knee-high monuments made of polished stone. Each had a brass plaque.

The first was dedicated to Captain John Horsley, the pilot that had been killed in the helicopter crash in the school grounds. The second was for Sharon Prentiss, one of the students.

The third was the reason he was here: Jael Marquez.

Jael had been Ryan's roommate, ever since he'd arrived at the school. Their relationship had been complicated: Jael couldn't deal with Ryan's attitude. He hated that he always got their dorm into trouble.

Ryan always found the kid irritating. Something

about Jael's voice and manner just grated on him. He was such a geek.

But now, Jael was dead.

And Ryan hadn't come to terms with that.

To be fair, he'd never had a chance.

After the accident, he'd been hurtling from one dangerous situation to another. It hadn't been a good time to process his loss.

'I'm sorry you died, Jael,' he said, feeling foolish talking to a stone. 'I know we didn't always get on, but I'm going to miss you.'

He felt nothing.

So, he just stood there.

He thought about the good times they'd shared. Time in the common room. Banter in the dorm. Projects they'd worked on together. The arguments they'd had.

As he recalled their last spat, his eyes welled up. He spoke again, his voice wavering. 'Devonmoor won't be the same without you, buddy. I'll never forget you.'

Just like that, the dam broke.

He fell on his knees and wept, overwhelmed by grief for his friend. He let it flow, his body racked with sobs.

And, in a strange way, he was relieved.

The tears confirmed his humanity; his emotion.

He wasn't a psychopath like the governor.

He wasn't evil like Conrad and Jasper Wolff.

He was Ryan Jacobs.

And he cared.

A NOTE FROM THE AUTHOR

Thanks for reading 'Hard Cell'. If you're up for more of Ryan's adventures, check out 'Cold Dawn' which is available now! In it, Ryan has to try to find the Fractal Processor before his enemies.

Maybe you'd also be interested in finding out about my new releases? If so, then my readers' club is the place to start! Visit www.paulorton.net to join.

And could you do me a huge favour? I need you to review 'Hard Cell'. Reviews on Amazon make a huge difference to a new author like me, and it would be amazing if you could write a sentence or two about what you liked about it. I'd really appreciate it and I promise I read <u>every</u> review.

Until next time,

Paul.

GET YOUR FREE E-BOOK

There are traps you can't escape.

When Ryan Jacobs asks to join the Faction he finds himself trapped in a situation which keeps getting worse. He needs to escape fast, or they will own him forever. But how can he fight an invisible enemy?

Find out about Ryan's life before he is taken to the Academy. DARK WEB is exclusively available to those in my readers' club – sign up for free at www.paulorton.net

RYAN JACOBS BOOK 6

They're coming for it. He doesn't have long.

Ryan is on the hunt for the Fractal Processor, but he's not alone. Unless he finds it first, the world could be in danger.

But Devonmoor Academy is a big place, and he barely has time to breathe. He can't tell anyone what he's up to, and he'll need to do things he'll later regret.

Is it worth risking everything to pay an old debt? Should he even try? Or is he about to hand over a dangerous weapon and make the biggest mistake of his life?

COLD DAWN is the sixth book in the Ryan Jacobs series and is <u>AVAILABLE NOW ON AMAZON</u>!

LOCKDOWN BOOK 1

They came for his family.
Now, they're after him.

Zac is on the run and there's nowhere to hide. The streets aren't safe and he can't evade the Quarantine Agency forever. Still, he made a promise he intends to keep.

Just how hard can it be to get across town during lockdown? And what will happen if he succeeds?

One thing's for sure: Zac wants answers.

But, more than that, he wants to live.

THE LAST HOPE OF LOCKDOWN is the first book of the Lockdown series and is <u>AVAILABLE NOW ON AMAZON!</u>

LOCKDOWN BOOK 2

They make the rules.
He breaks them.

Zac is a wanted boy. At thirteen, he's the youngest member of the Resistance, and about to become their most valuable asset. He's used to taking risks, but this latest mission will take him into enemy territory, unarmed and alone.

Now, he's feeling the pressure: if he fails, he'll let everyone down.

But it will be even worse for him.

THE RISE OF THE RESISTANCE is the second book of the Lockdown series and is <u>AVAILABLE NOW ON AMAZON!</u>

Printed in Great Britain
by Amazon

58334254R00118